GUARDED BY THE SHERIFF

MONIQUE DeVERE

LOVE INSPIRED SUSPENSE
INSPIRATIONAL ROMANCE

Recycling programs for this product may not exist in your area.

ISBN-13: 978-1-335-95785-6

Guarded by the Sheriff

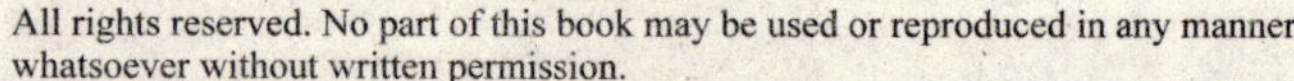

Love Inspired
22 Adelaide St. West, 41st Floor
Toronto, Ontario M5H 4E3, Canada
www.LoveInspired.com

HarperCollins Publishers
Macken House, 39/40 Mayor Street Upper,
Dublin 1, D01 C9W8, Ireland
www.HarperCollins.com

Printed in Lithuania

1 2 3 4 5 6 7 8 9 10 LIT 28 27 26 25

"Sienna, don't come any closer. It's a bomb."

She gasped, confusion knitting her expression. "A what?"

He knew she'd heard him, so he didn't repeat himself. "Take Nathan and get as far away from the truck as you can."

Without delay, she scooped Nathan into her arms and ran for the side of the house.

Ethan moved with them, positioning himself between them and the truck.

They had just reached the corner of the house when an explosion ripped through the truck behind them. They hit the ground hard, Ethan shielding Sienna and Nathan with his body.

Sienna screamed his name.

Nathan's petrified sobs tore at his heart.

"Are you hurt?" Ethan asked.

Sierra shook her head, still wide-eyed. "We're…" She ran a hand over Nathan, relief whooshing her breath from her lungs. "We're okay."

He got up, helping Sienna to her feet with Nathan clutched in her arms. "Take him inside. I'll call this in."

She nodded. Without hesitation, she turned and hurried with Nathan into the house.

Ethan reached for his phone, his gaze drifting back to the inferno blazing on the drive.

Something told him this was only the beginning…

Monique DeVere writes heart-pounding romantic suspense and funny, feel-good romances with heart, hope and a dash of sass. Her stories are filled with faith, emotional depth and unforgettable characters. Originally from Barbados, she lives in the UK with her real-life hero, their four children, five grandchildren and an adorable Yorkshire terrier. When she isn't writing, Monique enjoys family time, shell collecting, boating, being near the sea and learning something new.

Books by Monique DeVere

Love Inspired Suspense

Guarded by the Sheriff

Visit the Author Profile page at LoveInspired.com.

And I will restore to you the years
that the locust hath eaten.
—*Joel* 2:25

To my family, who remind me every day that love,
grace and forgiveness are the greatest gifts we
can give each other, and especially to my mum,
who never stopped encouraging me to hold on to
my dream of being published by Harlequin, and
who loved this book so much she read it twice
when it was still just a manuscript.

ONE

Sienna Blake pressed herself against the wooden stall, her heart hammering. The scent of warm hay and horse sweat filled the stable, mingling with the damp earthy aroma of trampled straw and old leather. From her hiding spot in the stallion's stall, she had a clear view of the two men arguing near the stable doors.

Trip Anderson, the ranch owner.

And a hulking stranger with a gun aimed at the elderly man.

Tension crackled in the air, thick and suffocating as the gunman's voice cut through the dimly lit stable block.

"You think you can cheat us?" The gunman stepped closer, his voice low, dangerous.

Trip held up both hands, taking a step backward. "It's not what you think. I just need more time."

"Time?" The gunman let out a low, humorless chuckle that sent ice slithering down Sienna's spine. "My boss doesn't do extensions."

Who was his boss?

Trip exhaled sharply. "Look, I know the foal's DNA could expose everything, but I'll fix it. I just need access to the system. Trina was supposed to take care of it."

Sienna frowned. Trina? The ranch's office manager? What did she have to do with the foal's DNA?

The gunman's expression hardened. "Trina messed up. The vet tech got suspicious. We had to clean that up."

Sienna's breath caught. *Clean it up? Did that mean...?*

Trip paled. "You—you killed Trina?"

Sienna clamped a hand over her mouth, forcing back a gasp. *Trina's dead?* Just a few days ago, she'd been gushing about her daughter's upcoming visit.

The gunman leaned in, his voice ice-cold. "And the vet tech. Consider it a warning. Do your job, or you're next, old man."

Trip swallowed hard, his shoulders sagging. "I never wanted any of this."

"No?" The gunman sneered. "Then maybe you shouldn't have taken the money."

What money? Did Trip borrow money he couldn't pay back, and now he was being forced to do something illegal? The gunman had mentioned the foal's DNA. Was Trip involved in falsifying bloodlines? Six years ago, while working as an equine physiotherapist on her father's ranch, she'd treated a stallion listed as an active breeder, but she knew he'd been sterile for years. Official records had claimed he'd fathered foals, but that was impossible. Then she'd discovered that someone had been altering bloodline records.

Trip's jaw clenched. "I just need to get through this week. If I can fix the papers, no one will ever question it."

"You better hope so." The gunman's voice dropped to a lethal tone. "Because if that DNA test goes through, the boss won't be waiting for you to fix it. He'll be cutting his losses."

Trip froze. "Wait, you're saying—"

The gunman pulled the slide back on his pistol. Pressed the barrel to Trip's chest, right over his heart. "You've got forty-eight hours. After that? You're just another loose end."

Trip staggered back, his face drained of color. Panic flashed in his eyes.

A loud whinny split the air. A horse stamped its hooves and shifted restlessly in the stall across from hers.

She kept her gaze on Trip. *He's going to do something reckless.*

The thought barely formed before Trip lunged. He grabbed for the gun, grappling with the man, but the guy was a foot taller and a truck-size wider.

A sharp pop cracked the air.

Trip stiffened.

The sickening thud of his body hitting the concrete floor sent icy prickles through Sienna.

A startled breath hitched in her throat. She clamped her lips shut, choking down a scream. She should run, but fear pinned her in place.

Trip wasn't moving. She willed him to get up. Run. Fight.

The four-year-old stallion beside her blew a sharp breath, ears flicking back as if he, too, were urging his owner to get up. Sienna edged to the stall door. Maybe she could sneak back out as unnoticed as when she arrived five minutes ago to collect her jacket. She took a slow step backward—and knocked against a metal bucket. It clattered to the ground, the sound like a gunshot in the silence.

The gunman's head snapped around.

And his cold, dark eyes locked on to hers.

Sienna's stomach plummeted. *No. No. No.* For a single, terrifying heartbeat, neither of them moved. Then he swung the gun in her direction, his finger tightening on the trigger.

A wave of terror slammed into her. Sienna squeezed her eyes shut. "Lord, help!"

A beat of silence.

Instead of a gunshot, she heard a click, then heavy footsteps. Her eyes flew open. The gunman was charging toward her, his face twisted with frustration as he tried to unjam his gun. In seconds he was blocking her exit.

His gun might've jammed, but she couldn't bank on it staying that way. Acting on instinct, she grabbed the lead rope hanging from the post and gave it a sharp tug. The stallion reared up, hooves slicing the air. The gunman's eyes widened as the horse's powerful legs kicked out, slamming into his chest. He grunted in pain, stumbled backward and crashed onto the straw-covered floor, his gun clattering out of his grip.

Oh, God, please help! Sienna didn't wait to see if the gunman got back up. Instead, she bolted, dodging past him, her boots skidding on the stable floor.

Nathan.

She'd only popped into the stables for a moment to grab the jacket she'd left while working with the stallion earlier. She hadn't meant to be here this long. And Nathan—her five-year-old son—was in the car just outside the stables.

Alone and vulnerable.

A wave of raw panic seized her. If the gunman recovered before she escaped, he wouldn't stop at taking her out. He'd find her son. Sienna pushed harder, sprinting toward the stable doors. Behind her, the man groaned. She risked a glance over her shoulder. He was already stirring. If she didn't get to Nathan first… She refused to finish the thought. She had to make it. Had to get to her son. Had to survive.

A second gunshot cracked the silence.

Pain slashed across her left arm. She stumbled. The force of the bullet's graze sent her crashing to her knees. She wrenched herself up, every instinct screaming to keep running. She had to escape. Had to stay alive. Had to protect Nathan.

She sprinted past Trip's lifeless body, burst through the stable doors and raced toward her car, ignoring the fiery sting in her arm. She fumbled for the door handle, her bloodied fingers slipping. Behind her, heavy footsteps pounded against the gravel, closing in.

Her heart slammed against her ribs, her heartbeat pounding in her ears. "Come on. Come on!" It took a couple of tries before she got the car door open. She dove behind the wheel, hands shaking as she pressed the button to start the ignition. The engine roared to life. Sienna slammed on the gas pedal.

A dark shape loomed in her peripheral vision—he was almost there.

The tires of her little car kicked up dirt and gravel as she peeled out of the driveway, the gunman's furious shout lost in the roar of the engine. Sienna glanced in the rearview mirror. Nathan was buckled into his booster seat, his Woody figure clutched in one hand as he stared out the back window.

"Mommy, is that a bad man?"

Her gaze shifted to the large man in the distance. Thank God he wasn't following. Right now, he probably had bigger problems with the ranch owner lying dead on the stable floor.

"Yes, peanut, that's a bad man."

"Don't let him get us, Mommy."

"I won't, baby." Dread formed a lump in her chest. She only prayed the big guy wasn't the type to finish what he started.

She kept one eye on the road, the other on the mirror. Nathan was safe—for now. But the knot in her chest tightened with every mile. What if this wasn't over? What if it was only the beginning?

Even with distance growing behind her, the danger still felt far too close.

Some days, Sheriff Ethan Callahan felt aged beyond his thirty-three years. Today was one of those days. He rolled his left shoulder, trying to ease the dull ache—a permanent souvenir of the day his life fell apart. The day he almost died. The day the woman he loved left town—left him—and never looked back. For months after the attempt on his life, he'd lived in dread that something had happened to Sienna, that whoever tried to kill him had gotten to her, too.

But they hadn't. Eventually, Ethan had found her—alive and well, continuing her work as an equine physiotherapist on a ranch in Idaho. She hadn't been running for her life. She'd been living it. Without him. Ethan had been forced to face the brutal truth—she hadn't left because she was in danger.

She'd left because she wanted to.

Because she didn't love him.

She'd abandoned him at his lowest point, when he'd needed her most. And if the way she'd run out on him wasn't enough of a lesson, then shame on him for still missing her.

He had once believed in God's plan. The day Sienna walked away—taking his heart—broke something inside him. The attack on his life had never been solved. The person responsible had walked free. He'd prayed for answers, for peace, for the woman he loved to return to him, but his prayers remained unanswered. In the end, he'd had to conclude that God wasn't hearing him. So why bother to pray?

"Please, I need to see him now."

The sudden commotion in the front office snapped Ethan out of his reverie. He pushed to his feet, his instincts on high alert. The tension in the woman's voice sent a ripple of unease through him. He stepped out of his office, his gaze landing on a slender woman a little above average height, her golden-brown hair gathered in a messy bun. It wasn't a cute, artfully arranged do. It was haphazard with curling strands falling out all over the place. Her face was devoid of makeup, and her clothes looked like she'd slept in them for days. And she was holding a little boy's hand, keeping him close as though she was afraid to let him out of her sight.

Ethan's breath stalled in his chest.

Sienna.

A wave of emotions crashed into him—shock, anger, disbelief. And beneath it all, something he refused to acknowledge. Something that made his stomach clench and his heart ache.

For six years, he'd convinced himself he would never see her again. That she had disappeared into another life without so much as a backward glance. And yet, here she was, standing in his sheriff's office, looking at him with wide, desperate hazel eyes.

The woman who had broken him. The woman he had once loved. The woman he had spent years trying to forget.

His gaze dropped to the boy. He looked about five or six, his small hand clinging to Sienna's, his tiny fingers curling tightly around hers as he stared back at Ethan with a mix of curiosity and wariness. The kid had dark hair, a strong jaw and the same stubborn tilt to his chin that Ethan saw every morning in the mirror.

His gut twisted. It couldn't be. But the resemblance was undeniable—so much so it made his knees lock. His heart slammed against his ribs. Was this why she ran out on him?

"Ethan." Sienna's voice wavered, and she maneuvered the boy closer as if to shield him from Ethan's reaction.

He forced himself to look at her, not the child who looked too much like him. Ethan's pulse roared in his ears, his anger a slow, simmering burn. But a wise man never jumped to conclusions and always kept control of his emotions.

"Sienna." Despite his effort to keep a grip on his reactions, his voice came out rough, barely more than a growl.

She took a hesitant step forward, her eyes pleading. "Please, Ethan. I didn't know where else to go."

And that was the only reason she came back. Not because she regretted leaving. Not because she missed him. But because she was out of options.

A fresh wave of anger surged, hot and blinding, but he locked it down before it took hold. He'd had years to build his defenses, to bury the part of himself that used to dream of this moment— of her return. But not like this.

Not standing in his office looking at him like he was her last hope.

Not with a child—his child?—clinging to her hand.

His chest tightened, the betrayal clawing the insides of his ribs like a beast desperate to get free. He had spent years trying to put her behind him, telling himself he was over her. But seeing her now, so familiar yet a stranger, made every raw, buried emotion crack open like a wound that never truly healed.

But he was a lawman first. His personal feelings didn't matter. Not right now.

Clearly, she wouldn't have returned to Hope Haven unless she was desperate. And that, more than anything, set his instincts on high alert.

"Come into my office." He indicated the way with a sweep of his hand as he glanced at Sally—the desk sergeant—who raised curious brows in return.

The door had barely clicked shut when the little boy spoke, his voice small and frightened. "Someone shot my mom."

Ethan's breath stilled.

The words hung in the air. His first instinct was to assess the threat. Someone had tried to kill Sienna? That meant she was in danger. Was the shooter still after her? Had she been followed? He scanned her again, this time with sharper focus—her pale face, the exhaustion in her eyes, the tension in her posture. She looked like a woman running on nothing but fear.

His gut clenched. *She's hurt.* The realization hit with brutal force, tamping the anger he'd barely managed to leash.

He took a controlled breath, forcing his body to stay calm when everything inside him told him to demand answers. Who did this? Why was she here? Why had she never told him about the boy? He shoved the last question aside. That wasn't the priority.

The child—wide-eyed and too still for a boy his age—was clinging to Sienna's hand like a lifeline. Fear radiated off him, and something inside Ethan shifted.

His job was to serve and protect. It didn't matter what had

happened between him and Sienna. Right now, she and this child—her child—needed him. He stepped closer, scanning her for injuries.

"Where are you hurt?" The question came out rougher than he intended, the simmering emotions threatening to rise again.

"It's just a graze. I'm fine." Her voice wavered, her hand shook, and even though she was putting on a brave face for the boy, Ethan could see that she was holding on by a thread.

His jaw locked. His fingers curled into fists. The thought of someone taking a shot at her—of nearly hitting their mark— tightened his chest. He exhaled sharply and forced himself to stay focused. "Let me see."

"It's only a scratch."

"Let me see anyway."

Sienna hesitated, but then she slowly unzipped her jacket, shrugging it down her arm to reveal a bandage beneath the sleeve of her pink T-shirt. The bandage looked clean, but the sight still sent a wave of heat rushing through him—anger, protectiveness and something he didn't dare name.

He exhaled, made an effort to steady his voice. "I'll call Doc Bennett to take a look. In the meantime, tell me everything. When did this happen?"

Sienna swallowed, righting her jacket. "Two days ago. In Idaho. I overheard something I shouldn't have." She glanced down at her son, clearly not wanting to speak freely in front of him.

He turned his gaze to the boy, who was still gripping Sienna's hand, his tiny fingers curled tightly around hers. The child had been silent, watching, his gaze flicking between them.

Ethan crouched to his level, softening his voice. "Hey, buddy. What's your name?"

The boy hesitated, then straightened his spine. "Nathan."

A fresh wave of emotion surged inside him, but he pushed it back. His feelings—the betrayal, the ache he didn't want to acknowledge—didn't matter right now. He nodded, keeping his expression gentle, even as his heart slammed against his ribs. *Nathan.*

Ethan looked into a pair of eyes identical to his own. "Is that short for Nathaniel?"

Nathan nodded.

With his index finger, he gently tapped the little boy's nose. "That's my middle name."

Nathan smiled. "We have the same name."

Over the little boy's head, Ethan stared into Sienna's over-bright hazel eyes. His heart and gut told him the truth. Sienna hadn't confirmed it yet, but deep in his spirit, he already knew. "Yes, we do."

He swallowed hard and forced himself to focus. Right now, protecting Sienna and their son was the priority. He couldn't let emotions cloud his judgment.

He met the little boy's blue gaze, softened his voice. "Nathan, would you like to go with Sally to the breakroom for a Popsicle?"

Nathan's little face lit up, his eyes shining with excitement, and he nodded vigorously.

Ethan's throat tightened. In the middle of all this fear and uncertainty, a Popsicle was all it took to bring the boy joy. He held out his hand, his heart almost cracking wide open when Nathan placed his tiny fingers in his. For a moment, Ethan couldn't move.

The warmth of that small hand—his son's hand—pressed into his palm, trusting, innocent, unaware of how profoundly the moment had just shaken Ethan to his core. How many moments like this had he already missed? How many more had been stolen from him? Pushing down the sudden ache in his chest, he guided Nathan to the outer office, conscious of how small and fragile that little hand felt in his own.

And even though Ethan's world had just been turned upside down, he knew one thing with absolute certainty.

He would protect this child with his life.

"I brought you coffee." Ethan reentered the office, two steaming mugs in his hands. The aroma of rich roasted coffee beans filled the space, wrapping around her like a familiar embrace. "Is it still black, no sugar?"

Sienna nodded, touched he remembered.

"Thanks." She accepted the mug—the one printed with butterflies. A small, unexpected kindness that made her throat tighten. The moment she'd seen him again, she'd wanted to throw herself into his strong arms, tell him how much she missed him. But the banked anger radiating off him had rooted her to the spot. If she'd imagined Ethan would welcome her with forgiveness, she knew now not to hope.

He placed his own mug—a plain black one—on his desk and folded his arms over his chest. "You were saying you overheard something you shouldn't have."

Sienna wrapped her fingers around her mug, craving the warmth that seeped into her hands. Inhaling deeply, she welcomed the comforting aroma that settled her nerves.

She should have been relieved to be here. Nathan was safe. But instead, a tangled knot of emotions gripped her.

Across the desk, Ethan stood statue-like—tall, steady, impenetrable. His presence filled the room, radiating strength... and tension.

This wasn't the Ethan she'd left behind. The laid-back charm, the easy laughter she used to love was gone. In its place stood a man hardened by time, his piercing blue eyes sharper, his jaw set firmly.

She took a slow breath, steeling herself. He was watching her, his expression unreadable.

Waiting.

She lifted her gaze, forcing herself to meet his eyes. "Trip, the ranch owner I work for, was arguing with a big, scary man I hadn't seen before."

Ethan didn't speak, but his sharp, unwavering focus sent her pulse skittering.

"I think Trip was involved in falsifying a bloodline." She put her mug on the desk, suddenly restless. "Apparently, one of the foal's DNA didn't match, and the people he was dealing with weren't happy. It looked like the guy was there to warn him."

Ethan's brow furrowed, but he stayed silent, letting her talk.

She hesitated. The memory still sent chills through her.

"Trip got spooked and rushed the gunman. The gun went off, and Trip was shot." Swallowing a rise of nausea, she forced herself to continue. "I tried to sneak out, but the gunman saw me." She shuddered at the memory. The way his cold eyes had locked on to hers. "I barely got away. I thought it was over, but that night, someone tried to break into my house."

Ethan went completely still, the air between them electric. And still, he didn't interrupt.

"Thankfully, the neighbor's dogs scared off the intruder. I packed a bag for me and Nathan, then left. I couldn't be sure I wasn't followed, so I took the long way here. Backtracked, changed routes, just in case."

Ethan's gaze never wavered nor softened.

And that hurt more than she was prepared for. But what had she expected? She didn't deserve his forgiveness. Not that he looked like he was considering it.

Ethan's expression didn't change, but something flickered in his eyes—something she couldn't quite name. "You and Nathan are staying with me."

She should argue. Should tell him she didn't need a bodyguard—that she could protect herself. But they both knew that would be a lie. She had been running, surviving on coffee and gas station sandwiches. Fearing for her son's safety.

Nathan needed protection. And if there was one person in this world she trusted to keep him safe, it was Ethan. She swallowed past the lump in her throat and forced herself to meet his gaze.

"Okay."

Half an hour later, after Doc Bennett had examined her arm and agreed she didn't need stitches, they were on their way. Ethan had transferred the things from her car to his patrol truck before securing her car in the lockup. Now they were heading to his ranch, the steady hum of the engine filling the silence between them. Outside, the Montana landscape stretched for miles—rolling fields dusted in twilight, the distant silhouette of the mountains standing like silent sentinels against a sky dotted with the first stars of the evening.

Ethan's hands gripped the wheel, his jaw set tight.

Sienna could feel the weight of everything left unsaid pressing between them.

Nathan, curled up in his booster seat behind them, had finally drifted off, exhaustion claiming him.

She folded her hands in her lap, stealing a glance at Ethan's profile.

Strong. Stubborn. Silent.

This man had once been her whole world. Now, he was a stranger sitting beside her, one she had hurt more than anyone else.

She cleared her throat, needing to break the silence. "Thank you."

Ethan didn't look at her. "For what?"

She hesitated. *For everything. For protecting Nathan. For not turning me away.* But those words felt too raw, so she settled on, "For letting us stay with you."

Ethan exhaled. The tension between them thickened until the air felt too heavy to breathe. "Were you ever going to tell me?"

He didn't have to clarify. She knew exactly what he meant.

Her fingers curled into her lap, shame coiling in her stomach. "Yes."

Ethan's gaze remained fixed on the road, but the weight of his disbelief pressed against her.

"When?" His voice was low, controlled, but she heard the anger buried beneath the restraint. The quiet demand scraped against her raw nerves.

She stared down at her tightly clasped hands. "I don't know." A thousand different answers tangled on her tongue. She didn't know where to begin. "I wanted to."

Ethan glanced at her. Even in the dimming light she recognized the storm in his eyes. "What stopped you?"

"It's a long story."

He cut her a glance. "I have all night."

She turned her gaze to the window. "It started with a stallion on my father's ranch that had been listed as an active breeder. But he'd been sterile for years. When I—"

Blinding headlights appeared out of nowhere, barreling toward them. A sharp, cold terror seized her. A blaring horn ripped through the night, a deafening sound as the eighteen-wheeler veered into their lane, coming straight for them.

Her heart slammed against her ribs.

"Ethan—"

She couldn't even hear her own voice over the horn. All she could do was brace for impact and pray they'd survive it.

TWO

The monstrous rig bore down on them, horn blaring, metal gleaming, its sheer force vibrating through Ethan's patrol truck.

His stomach dropped. He jerked the wheel hard to the left, tires screeching as the SUV veered into the oncoming lane. If another car came around the bend, they'd be trapped in the head-on collision he was trying to avoid. But his choices were bad, worse or catastrophic—swerve and hope the road was clear, stay put and collide head-on with the semi, or slam into the guardrail and plummet into the ravine below.

The road ahead was clear. Relief barely registered before the semi swerved back into their path.

Straight at them.

With a hard right, his SUV lurched back into their lane. The semi jumped lanes again.

Beside him, Sienna clutched the dashboard, frantically praying over them, her voice low and tremulous. He was no longer a praying man, but right now, he had no problem with her calling on divine intervention.

Sienna gasped. "Ethan, there's no one driving that truck!"

His gaze shot to the cab. She was right. The driver's seat was empty. Self-driving semis were becoming more common, but this one was on the wrong side of the road.

A malfunction?

He swerved again, tires squealing in protest. The semi followed. Gut churning, he shifted back into the right lane. The eighteen-wheeler mirrored him—barreling toward them, seconds from impact. He took another evasive maneuver. He'd never been more thankful for that advanced driving course than he was right now. The guardrail loomed to his right—a thin barrier between them and a deadly drop. One wrong move and—he couldn't let himself go there. His grip tightened.

"Hold on." He angled toward the narrow strip of land beside the semi, his sole focus on keeping them from going over. The screech of metal against guardrail was deafening as the patrol truck squeezed past the semi on the inside. Up ahead, the guardrail was gone. He hit the brakes, but the tires clipped loose gravel, and suddenly, the ground vanished beneath them.

The SUV lurched sideways, plunging down the slope, crashing through underbrush as gravity yanked them downward. The vehicle tilted forward, the headlights sweeping across jagged terrain.

Sienna let out a choked cry as they skidded down the embankment, bouncing over uneven ground. "Dear God, save us!"

Nathan's terrified cry rang from the back seat.

Ethan fought the steering wheel, determined to keep them from flipping. Branches scraped against metal. Rocks pelted the undercarriage. The tires clawed at the crumbling ground, but momentum dragged them.

The patrol truck bucked over a dip in the terrain, then slammed hard with bone-jarring force. Sliding down the embankment at a stomach-lurching angle, the truck fishtailed as Ethan fought for control, dirt and gravel kicking up like a dust storm.

He wrestled the vehicle, braking hard against gravity's terrifying pull. If they tipped sideways, it was over. Abruptly, the rear tires snagged on something solid, jerking them to a gutpunching stop.

For a long, breathless moment, the patrol truck teetered precariously. The pungent mineral scent of dust and clay mingled with crushed pine needles and burnt rubber permeated the SUV's interior. Ethan's stomach turned to lead. He hardly dared to breathe. His foot jammed hard on the brake kept the vehicle steady. He flexed his hands against the wheel, heart hammering. They had seconds before the ground shifted.

Beside him, Sienna's breath came in shallow, panicked gasps, her fingers clutching the dashboard in a death grip.

In the back, Nathan whimpered.

Ethan slowly, carefully reached out, easing Sienna back in her seat. A tremor racked her, her hands shaking as she finally uncurled her fingers from the dashboard. She turned to him, breath shaky. "Ethan?"

"Don't move." He cautiously turned his head to check on Nathan. The child was shaking with terror, his face wet with tears. Ethan turned his gaze to Sienna and lowered his voice to a murmur to avoid Nathan hearing. "The front tires are almost over the edge."

Just beyond the hood, the ground vanished into a steep drop-off and a jagged boulder ravine.

Sienna pressed a trembling hand over her mouth. "Oh, God, please help. Don't let us die like this," she whispered.

"Mommy, are we going to die?" Nathan's fractured voice tore at Ethan's heart.

Sienna exhaled shakily, reaching back awkwardly to stroke a comforting hand on her son's little leg. "No, baby boy. God has us, remember?"

"I'm scared, Mommy."

Ethan had only known of Nathan's existence for an hour, but an instinctive protectiveness surged through him, shocking him in its intensity. The fear in Nathan's voice sparked a deep, primal urge to protect stronger than anything he'd ever expected.

"Close your eyes." Sienna's tone might've been calm for

her son's sake, but her terror was tight on her face. "Are they closed?"

"Yes," Nathan whimpered.

"Good. Now, picture the big bowl of ice cream you'll have when we get out of here." She met Ethan's eyes. He couldn't tell whether she believed that or if she was simply trying to pacify her child. "Can you see it?"

"Yes." Another snuffle.

"What flavor is it?"

While she distracted Nathan, Ethan shifted into 4WD Low and eased into Reverse. The 4×4 system would transfer power to the rear tires, giving them more traction on the uneven ground.

He pressed gently on the gas, carefully rocking the truck. Any sudden movement would send them over. The rocky outcrop offered just enough grip for the tires to gain traction. Loose gravel skittered over the edge, but slowly the tires found solid purchase. Ethan continued a controlled reverse back up the embankment.

Finally, the front wheels cleared the edge. He maintained steady pressure until they crested safely back onto stable ground. Breath trapped somewhere between his lungs and throat, hands locked on the wheel, every muscle bunched tight, he waited for the world to stop tilting.

That hadn't been an accident.

Someone had just tried to kill them.

When they finally reached the road, Sienna could have wept with relief.

"Stop the car." She couldn't breathe properly, couldn't think clearly. Not until she held Nathan in her arms. Her heart thundered, fear still vibrating through every nerve. Her child's broken voice calling out to her, scared and vulnerable, kept replaying in her mind. She had to hold him close, assure herself that he was unharmed. Ethan pulled over, glancing at her with concern. But she barely noticed. Her trembling fingers fumbled with the seat belt, desperate urgency making her movements clumsy. The SUV hadn't fully stopped moving before she unbuckled her seat belt, shoved the door open and jumped out onto the shoulder.

She yanked open the back door, tears burning.

Nathan stared at her with wide, frightened eyes, cheeks still damp, body trembling.

He's alive. My sweet baby is alive.

She climbed into the back seat and released his booster seat buckle with shaking fingers. "Come here, baby."

Nathan launched into her arms, burying his face in her neck, and his little hands gripped her desperately. She wrapped him tightly in her embrace, breathing him in, savoring the warmth of his small body pressed against her chest.

Silent tears spilled down her cheeks as relief overwhelmed her.

Thank You, Lord. Thank You for protecting him. For protecting all of us.

"It's okay," she whispered into Nathan's silky hair, smoothing a comforting hand over his back. "I've got you."

As she clung to her little boy, she registered Ethan's steady voice talking into the radio mic.

"Dispatch, this is Sheriff Callahan. Be advised, we've encountered a rogue unmanned semi actively targeting vehicles on the northbound stretch of Highway 89 near mile marker 17. Vehicle is highly dangerous, possibly sabotaged. Request immediate backup, traffic diversion and aerial support if possible. Advise responding units to intercept with extreme caution."

Dispatch crackled acknowledgment.

He continued, his voice firm. "I'm transporting civilians to a secure location. Deputy Carter, you're lead on scene. Handle with caution and keep me updated."

Ethan returned the mic to its cradle, his gaze meeting hers

in the rearview mirror. She tightened her arms around Nathan, her heart aching that he'd already experienced so much trauma at such a young age.

Had someone deliberately tried to kill them, or was this just a terrible accident?

As if reading her mind, Ethan's jaw tightened. A chill slipped down her spine. Had she set this nightmare in motion two days ago when she overheard Trip arguing with that man? Or had it begun six years earlier, the day she confronted her father about his role in falsifying that racehorse's bloodline?

"Ready?" Ethan's deep voice drew her back.

She nodded, reluctantly easing Nathan from her arms and buckling him securely into his seat. She took a deep breath as she fastened her own seat belt and braced herself for whatever came next.

Fifteen minutes later, Ethan pulled onto a gravel driveway. The SUV's headlights swept across a white split-rail fence framing the ranch's entrance. Tall wooden posts supported the rustic gate, marked with the Callahan name carved deeply into the wood. The fence line stretched into darkness on either side, outlining the boundary of Ethan's property.

Crossing through the gate felt symbolic, like stepping out of danger and into safety. Sienna leaned forward, pulse quickening as the ranch came into view. "You bought the old Landry place?"

Ethan glanced at her through the rearview mirror, his expression softening slightly. "Yeah. Carl and Betty sold it about three years ago to move closer to their kids."

Warm memories washed over her as the familiar log-and-stone house emerged from the shadows, bathed in soft golden lights. Its sprawling porch and large windows offered a warmth and protection she hadn't realized she desperately craved. More lights flickered on as they drew closer, washing gently over a barn that stood tall and solid, the weathered wood a testament to years of Montana's harsh winters.

Carl and Betty Landry had been kind, generous people, welcoming everyone who visited with fresh coffee, homemade pie and the kind of entertaining conversation that made anyone feel instantly at home. Growing up on her own family's expansive ranch, Sienna had appreciated the intimacy and warmth of the Landrys' smaller, quieter place.

Ethan had clearly worked hard to preserve the heart of the property, evident in the thoughtful placement of lights illuminating the barn, porch and surrounding pastures. Beyond the reassuring glow, the rest of Ethan's ranch was cloaked in shadows. She could just make out the outlines of fenced paddocks and the pastures, edged by jagged silhouettes of towering pines against the moonlit sky.

Everything about Ethan's home spoke of warmth, security, permanence. It was like a sanctuary, and right now, she needed that more than ever. "It still feels warm and inviting."

Their gazes briefly connected in the mirror, sharing something gentle yet unspoken before Ethan's eyes hardened and he turned his attention back to the driveway.

"Thanks. I wanted to honor what the Landrys built here." He brought the SUV to a stop near the foot of the porch steps.

Sienna released herself from the seat belt, then unbuckled Nathan.

"Let's get the two of you inside, then I'll grab your things." Ethan got out of the vehicle and Sienna followed. She lifted her son into her arms, her heart pinching when he wrapped his thin arms and legs around her and held on tight.

"It's okay," she whispered into Nathan's ear as she followed Ethan up the porch steps. "You're safe now."

"With Sheriff Callahan?" he whispered back, a hint of hero worship in his small voice.

Sienna glanced ahead at Ethan's broad shoulders, solid and

reassuring beneath the uniform he wore so naturally. Tall and commanding, he embodied strength and protection—exactly the kind of person anyone would long to have watching over them. A wave of embarrassment swept over her at how easily his quiet strength calmed her fears, even when logic told her not to depend on him.

"Yes." She hugged her son tighter. "With Sheriff Callahan."

Ethan opened the heavy wooden door and ushered them inside.

The warm comforting scent of something delicious cooking in the oven met them, and Sienna inhaled deeply. It felt like weeks instead of days since she last had a home-cooked meal. Then a possibility she hadn't considered knotted her stomach. While Ethan was at work, someone was here at his house preparing his dinner, probably anticipating his arrival as she once had.

She'd rushed to Hope Haven, never considering for a second that Ethan might've moved on. She hadn't even checked to see if he was wearing a ring, hadn't asked him anything about his life. He'd bought the Landrys' ranch. Had it been to start a family with a new wife?

An unseen fist squeezed her heart, and her stomach gave a sickening flip. "Ethan, Nathan and I can stay at a guesthouse. I don't want to intrude."

He paused in stepping back outside. She glanced at his left hand holding the door. No ring, but that didn't mean anything. Not everyone chose, or was able, to wear jewelry.

His dark brows drew together. "How would you be intruding?"

"Well…" Her face stung all the way from her neck to her hairline. "I wouldn't want your wife to think—"

"My *wife*?" His eyebrows shot up. "What makes you think I have a wife, Sienna?"

"Someone's cooking."

He made an *Ahh, right* face. "My mother. She insists on making sure I eat."

"Grace?"

"Yep, that's the one. She's probably in the kitchen. You can go say hello. I'm sure she'd be thrilled to see you again and meet little Nathan."

For some reason, that last part made her knees wobble. "Do you mind if we clean up first?"

"Sure." He jerked his chin toward the hallway. "Choose whichever rooms you prefer. Fresh linen is in the cupboard." With that, he turned and jogged lightly down the porch steps.

Sienna stood rooted to the spot. She wasn't ready to face Grace yet. The woman must hate her for the way she left Ethan while he lay injured in the hospital. And Nathan… She'd take one look at the little boy and know immediately.

Just as Ethan had.

Sienna glanced around her surroundings. Honey-colored walls glowed softly in the golden lamplight, creating an inviting atmosphere. A stone fireplace——clearly built to withstand harsh mountain winters——anchored the spacious living room and was surrounded by plush leather couches and solid hand-crafted wooden furniture that appeared sturdy enough to last generations.

She finally forced her feet to take her down the hall, the wide-planked hardwood floor creaking softly beneath her steps. Wood-carved lamps, black-and-white photos of Montana landscapes and shelves filled with books added character, reminding her of the man Ethan was. A man who valued solitude, history and peace.

"Hey, Nate, how about a bath?" It was late, and she really should get him to bed, but she couldn't bring herself to let him out of her sight just yet. She'd bought him dinner before they'd gone to see Ethan, so he wasn't hungry, but she had promised him ice cream, and she never made promises she didn't keep.

Nathan's head rested on her shoulder. He let out a loud, pretend snore.

Sienna smiled. "Oh dear... Nathan's fallen asleep. I guess he won't be having that ginormous bowl of ice cream after all."

Nathan's head shot up, his grin a balm to her soul. "I'm awake! I'm awake!"

Sienna tickled him, loving his sweet little-boy giggle. "You are, are you?"

She held on to the sound, tucking it into the quiet ache in her chest. Because moments like this were everything—and far too easy to lose.

After unloading Sienna's bags from the truck and carrying them to the room she'd chosen, Ethan stepped onto the porch and pulled his cell phone from his pocket. With tension coiling tight in Ethan's gut, he dialed Deputy Jack Carter.

Carter picked up immediately. "Sheriff?"

"What's happening with the semi?"

"It's gone." Carter blew out a breath, frustration clear in his voice. "We searched the entire stretch of highway. It's like the thing vanished—no sign, no trace. Almost as if it were never there."

Unease prickled up Ethan's spine. "That's impossible. I saw it with my own eyes. It ran us off the road." He rubbed the back of his neck, trying to erase the uneasy prickle.

"Us?"

Ethan shifted, suddenly restless. "Sienna, her son and me."

"Sienna?"

"Don't go there, Carter." Ethan pinched the bridge of his nose, attempting to ease the building pressure. He and Jack had been friends for fifteen years. They'd been through a lot together, including the day someone walked up behind Ethan and shot him in the back. Carter had saved his life that day, but he didn't get to ask questions about Sienna.

"Okay, okay." Ethan could picture his deputy raising a hand in that familiar gesture of retreat. "But right now, there's nothing to prove that semi even existed."

"It couldn't have just disappeared. Someone must've seen something. Check traffic cameras, Carter."

"I'm on it. We'll keep looking until we get answers."

Ethan raked a hand through his hair, frustration gnawing at his insides. "Keep me posted."

"Sure thing."

Ethan ended the call, exhaling slowly as he stared into the quiet darkness beyond the porch. The semitruck had vanished without a trace, leaving a lingering unease that crawled beneath his skin.

Still, that discomfort paled compared to the turmoil stirred by Sienna's sudden return after six long years.

Seeing her again had knocked him sideways. She'd always had the power to dismantle his defenses, and clearly, nothing had changed. She still held a piece of him he'd never managed to reclaim, despite years of trying. And now, with danger looming over her and Nathan, all those carefully buried emotions surged uncomfortably back to the surface.

Watching her care so tenderly for Nathan, a son he hadn't even known existed until today, stirred a painful mix of longing and regret.

The soft murmur of crickets filling the spring night reminded him that life had moved forward, even if part of him hadn't.

The front door opened, drawing Ethan's attention.

His mom stepped onto the porch and offered him a gentle smile. "I left dinner for you—herb-roasted chicken, garlic mashed potatoes, vegetables and fresh rolls."

"Thanks, Mom. I'm sorry I haven't been in to see you. I've got a situation."

She glanced back at the door. "So I see." She reached up to hug him.

Ethan wrapped his arms around her, drawing comfort from her familiar warmth.

Pulling back, she lightly touched his cheek. "There's plenty for two."

"Mom, I—"

"It's okay." She patted his cheek, eyes crinkling with understanding. "When you're ready."

A flush warmed his neck. His mother always saw more than he intended to reveal. "Thanks, Mom. Drive safely."

She smoothed his shirt collar. "Good night, Ethan."

"Night, Mom."

As she drove away, Ethan turned back toward the warm glow spilling from the house. Sienna was in there—scared, vulnerable and holding answers he wasn't sure he was ready to hear. She needed his protection, but could he trust her?

The past had returned tonight. And sooner or later, they'd have to face it.

THREE

After his bath, Sienna dressed Nathan in fresh pj's from the bag of his things she'd found just inside the bedroom door. Ethan had clearly slipped into the room to drop them off while Nathan was in the bath.

She'd grabbed a quick shower and washed her hair, only to find Nathan fast asleep by the time she came out. Quietly, she made him comfortable, whispered a prayer over him, then checked the window locks before stepping into the hallway. She could only delay the inevitable for so long before she had to face Ethan…and the past.

The comforting scent of roasted chicken, herbs and fresh bread guided her to the kitchen where she found him, sleeves rolled up, a blue checked tea towel draped over one shoulder as he plated food with a quiet efficiency that made her pause. The soft clink of cutlery against ceramic and the hum of the refrigerator were the only sounds in the room, and for a moment she just watched him—this strong, steady man she'd once loved with her whole heart. Who probably hated her now.

He glanced over his shoulder and did a quick double take when he saw she was alone. "Nathan?"

She pulled the sleeves of her soft cardigan down over her hands. "He's out like a light. He crashed while I was in the shower."

Ethan raised an eyebrow. "He went to bed without dinner?"

What kind of mother did he think she was?

"He ate earlier before we stopped at your office." On second thought, if she told him she'd fed their son fast food, he'd definitely think her a terrible mom, even if it had been from Nathan's favorite restaurant.

Ethan nodded, then gave a small smile as he reached for another plate. "Guess the ice cream didn't make the cut."

Sienna forced a smile, unable to hide the sadness weighing her down. "The day caught up with him. He's exhausted."

"Can't blame him." He paused in dishing chicken, mashed potatoes, and vegetables onto the plate. He gave her a sympathetic glance. "It's been a big day for you, too."

She didn't want to think about the day she'd had, and the sympathy in Ethan's gaze had her blinking back tears. Now was not the time to dissolve, not when she had to stay vigilant.

Motioning to the sturdy chalk-painted table in the center of the room, he silently invited her to sit as he placed the warmed plates on the placemats.

She glanced around the kitchen. The space was wide and functional, yet cozy like it had been when the Landrys owned the ranch. Knotty oak cabinets lined the walls, and cast-iron pans hung from a rack above the stove. The countertops were a dark polished stone, and the wide double farmhouse sink beneath the window sparkled.

Sienna slid into the chair, more famished than she wanted to admit. She hadn't eaten with Nathan—she'd been too keyed up, too anxious to get to Hope Haven. "Dinner looks amazing. Thank you."

"No problem. Mom made plenty, and I don't mind sharing."

Sienna inhaled the mouthwatering aroma wafting up from her plate. "Thanks."

He nodded, flicking the tea towel from his shoulder and depositing it on the countertop.

She reached for her cutlery as Ethan settled into his seat opposite her. "Where's Grace?"

He offered his hand for her to take, palm open, and bowed his head.

"I meant your mom."

His grin told her he knew she was asking about his mom and not about saying grace before they ate.

Despite the tension knotting her muscles, she found herself chuckling. She'd forgotten his sense of humor. She placed her hand in his, shocked by the spark of energy that shot up her arm at the contact and the fact he still had that effect on her.

After saying grace, he passed her the bread basket. "Mom went home."

Sienna selected a roll, still warm from the oven, and pinched off a bite, grateful for the distraction of food. "I'm sorry I missed her."

He threw her a skeptical glance. "Really?"

He'd always been too good at reading her. She drew in a steadying breath, setting the roll down on her plate. "She must hate me."

Ethan cut into his chicken but kept his attention on her, making her feel exposed. "'Hate' is a strong word, Sienna. Mom doesn't hate you."

She looked down at her plate. "Do you?" She forced herself to meet his eyes. "Hate me, that is."

His fork lingered in the air halfway to his mouth. "I thought I did. You left without a word, Sienna. I waited months. Years. For you to come back. And when you finally did, you were towing a child. *My* child that I didn't know existed. Not until today."

He couldn't possibly know for certain that Nathan was his, but why even go there? A blind person could see the resemblance and easily pick father and son out from a packed crowd.

She said nothing. What could she say? *I'm sorry* seemed so pathetically lacking. He was right. She'd vanished without warning. And now here she was—dropped back into his life with a son who looked so much like him it hurt to see them side by side.

Leaving had been the only way to save him. Now, she'd brought the threat straight to his door. If nothing else, she owed him an explanation. Not that she expected him to forgive her. Keeping his son from him was unforgivable.

Sienna wasn't sure *she* could ever forgive herself.

They ate in heavy silence—the kind that hung between two people with a complicated history—the air thick with tension. Every scrape of a fork or clink of a glass seemed amplified.

Her fingers fidgeting with her bread roll, she glanced at him. "I didn't know I was pregnant when I left."

His gaze narrowed, the blue irises darkening. "It clearly didn't matter, because when you found out, you stayed gone."

Her throat tightened, and she looked away before emotion could betray her. "I had to go, Ethan. I didn't want to leave you, but I had no choice."

His jaw ticked. "You always have a choice, Sienna. Did someone have a gun to your head?"

"In a manner of speaking, yes." Absently pushing the chicken around her plate with her fork, she drew in a deep breath. "When I was working on my father's ranch, I came across some paperwork—breeding schedules, registry logs, that sort of thing. I noticed inconsistencies. At first, I thought they were just careless mistakes. But there were too many. Foals listed under mares that were never bred. A stallion registered as active even though he'd been sterile for years. Whole bloodlines…fabricated.

"And then there were the payments. Large sums transferred to private accounts, disguised as consulting fees." She glanced up to find Ethan watching her with an intensity that made her pulse thud in her throat. "I asked my dad if he was involved in bloodline fraud. He told me to forget what I saw. Said it was bigger than both of us. That if I didn't keep my mouth shut, I'd bring down more trouble than I could imagine."

She blew out a shaky breath. "But I didn't back off. I told him I couldn't ignore it. That night, I got a call from an unknown number. I didn't recognize the voice, but it was a man. He told me to leave town if I wanted to see you alive again."

She tried to keep her tone neutral, but it broke as she whispered, "Even then, I wasn't afraid. Because I knew I'd go to you, and together, we'd stop whoever was behind it."

"So what happened? Why didn't you come to me?" Ethan's voice cut through the tension, rough with barely restrained anger.

"I told the man on the other end of the line that I wasn't going anywhere. The next day, you were in surgery fighting for your life." Her voice hitched. "I got another call from the same number. This time, he made it clear the attempt on your life was just a warning shot. And if I didn't leave town and keep my mouth shut, the next one would be fatal. I couldn't risk your life."

She laid her fork on the edge of her plate. There was no way she could get even a tiny morsel past the knot in her throat. "I thought if I disappeared…if I left town…they'd leave you alone."

He sat in silence, staring past her, absorbing it all. Then he looked at her, voice so quiet it sent shivers through her. "You should've told me. We could've figured it out together."

"No, Ethan. They would've *killed* you. I couldn't risk that. I never would've been able to live with myself if you died because of something I did."

Having stopped eating, he pushed his plate away. His eyes searched her face as if trying to decide whether he could believe her.

"And now? Why come back now?"

The air between them went still.

She pushed her damp hair back off her face. "Because I've put Nathan in danger. And his father is the only man I trust to protect him."

The bright hazel eyes staring back at him seemed almost too big for her face. He couldn't look at her for long—not when his heart still ached in places only she had touched. And yet, the sincerity in those golden-green depths pulled him in. He'd promised himself he wouldn't let her do that. But the second he saw fear flicker in her gaze, something primal stirred in him. Not just as a sheriff, but as a man who had once loved her.

She looked wary, worn out from everything she'd been through, and yet still so achingly familiar. Her freshly scrubbed face made her look younger than thirty, and the damp curls of her golden-brown hair flattered her delicate features. Black jeans hugged her slender legs. They were paired with boots, a white long-sleeved tee and a long peach cardigan that softened her in a way he hadn't expected.

He exhaled slowly, raking a hand through his hair. "You trust me to protect him but not enough to tell me he existed?" He rubbed the back of his neck. "I'm still trying to wrap my head around the fact that I have a five-year-old son asleep down the hall."

Sienna's lips parted, but no sound came. Her gaze dropped to her barely touched plate.

Ethan lowered his voice, but couldn't disguise the edge. "I keep thinking about everything I missed. His first steps. His first words. The sleepless nights, the tantrums, the cuddles. I didn't get to be his father. I wasn't given the chance."

Tears welled in her eyes. "I'm so sorry."

"I'm not saying that to hurt you, Sienna." He wasn't sure what hurt more: that she'd kept the truth from him or that part of him still wanted to reach across the table and take her hand.

She wiped her palms along the thighs of her jeans. "This is

your chance to be his father. I will never be able to atone for what I did, Ethan, but please believe me, I did it to protect you and Nate."

"Six years, Sienna." His voice came out rougher than he intended. "You stayed away for six years. I can understand a few months…but *years*?"

The tears brimming on her lashes spilled down her face. She brushed them away as if ashamed by the crack in her composure. "I was scared, and then…"

"And then?"

She bit her lip, looking so vulnerable it pinched his heart. "I was afraid that you'd reject me…and our child."

Unable to sit still any longer, he stood and gathered their plates. "Is that the type of man you think I am?"

She shook her head, mouth opening and closing as though she were trying to form the words but couldn't.

He crossed to the sink and deposited the plates before bracing his hands on the counter, staring out into the night, making no effort to fill the silence that stretched between them. Then he turned. "I don't know if I can ever forgive you…but I will protect our son with everything I have."

Sienna's breath hitched as she nodded. "That's all I ask."

Ethan leaned back against the counter and folded his arms across his chest as if it could shield him from the pull she still had. He didn't want to feel anything. And definitely not the ache that came from just being near her. "You need to understand how surreal this is. You show up—just as suddenly as you left—with a child, and possibly someone trying to kill you, and I don't even know why."

"I told you why." Her voice trembled as she wrapped the soft cardigan tightly around herself like a protective blanket. "I witnessed Trip's murder. And I overheard them talking about a foal's DNA. It doesn't take a master detective to figure out Trip was involved in bloodline fraud."

Ethan shifted his weight, the tension in his shoulders refusing to ease. "Do you have any proof?"

Sienna shook her head. "Not hard evidence. Just what I overheard at Trip's ranch—and what I saw at my father's. I'm almost certain they were both involved in the same racehorse bloodline scheme. Trip wouldn't have had access to those rare bloodlines without someone like my dad backing him. I could go to Dad's ranch, but now that he's gone, I don't know if any of the paperwork is still around."

It had been nearly a year since her father's heart attack. Ethan had expected her to return for the funeral. When she hadn't, he'd known then—if her father's death couldn't bring her back to Hope Haven, nothing would. Certainly not him.

"Your uncle took over the ranch after your dad, Jacob, passed, didn't he?"

She reached for her water glass, her fingers curling around it like she needed the anchor. "So I'm told. Dad left everything to Uncle Mason…and just enough for Mom to move to Florida."

Of course he had. Jacob Blake had always been calculated, even in death.

"How's your relationship with Mason?"

A small shrug lifted her shoulders. "He's my favorite uncle, but I haven't spoken to him in a while."

That didn't surprise Ethan. She'd cut ties with everyone when she left, including the people who might've helped her.

"Do you think he'd let you look at any of your dad's old records? Anything that might still be at the ranch?"

Her hesitation was brief, but he noticed it. She hadn't been back to her father's ranch since before Jacob died. Going there might stir memories—grief—she wasn't ready to face. And if she and Mason hadn't spoken since she left Hope Haven, maybe she wasn't sure of the kind of reception she'd get. "I can ask."

Ethan pushed away from the counter, needing to move, to do

something with the restless energy building inside him. Pacing to the far end of the kitchen near the mudroom, he turned back.

"We'll need proof of wrongdoing, Sienna. Something solid."

Her gaze dropped to the water glass, lashes casting shadows against her cheeks.

"Dad's not here to face the consequences of his part in the fraud."

No, he wasn't. But someone else was still pulling the strings. Someone who didn't hesitate to hurt anyone who got in the way.

"Like you said, this is bigger than Jacob. And whoever's behind it, we need to take them down."

She nodded, her eyes lifting to meet his. She wasn't just beautiful; she was brave, and that undid him a little.

"I'll call Uncle Mason in the morning."

He saw the flicker of uncertainty in her eyes. She'd been through enough. But she wasn't alone anymore.

Someone had forced her to run. Had tried to silence her. Had nearly taken his life.

His jaw clenched.

Now, after six long years, he'd finally have the chance to bring the person who tore their lives apart to justice.

A child's terrified scream jerked Sienna awake.

Her heart slammed against her ribs as she sat up in the dark. "Nathan?" Her hand flew out, searching blindly.

He was already clutching her arm, his little body shaking. "He was here." His panicked voice, choked with fear, pierced through her sleep-fogged brain. "The bad man was here. He was gonna put a pillow on your face!"

She yanked him into her arms and held him close. "Shh… baby, it's okay. You're safe. It was just a dream. You had a nightmare, that's all."

But Nathan shook his head wildly, anguished tears spilling down his cheeks. "No, Mommy. It was real…not a dream. He was here. He was standing right there." He pointed frantically toward her side of the bed.

Sienna's breath caught.

Tightening her hold on him, her gaze darted to the spot he indicated. The bedroom door stood wide open.

She was almost certain she'd closed it when she came to bed. Hadn't she? By the time she'd finished her prayers, exhaustion had pulled her under before her head even hit the pillow.

The moonlight filtering through the curtains cast a faint glow over the room but revealed nothing. No figure. No movement. No sign that anyone had been there.

Still, a chill crept down her spine.

Kissing the top of Nathan's head, her hand stroked his silky hair, but he remained nearly inconsolable. The ragged sobs kept coming, broken and breathless.

"You're safe now, peanut. Mommy's here. No one's going to hurt you."

The words sounded hollow, even to her.

Over the noise of Nathan's distress, she hadn't heard a single thing. If someone had been in the room, his cries could have covered any unusual sounds.

A shadow filled the doorway.

Sienna startled, then released a shaky breath when she recognized Ethan's silhouette. His expression was tense, his voice low.

"I heard him scream. What happened?"

Nathan buried his face against her neck, his small body trembling with every hiccupped sob. "Th-the bad man…was h-here!"

Sienna met Ethan's eyes, fighting to keep her voice steady. "He said someone was standing beside the bed. That he was going to hurt me."

Nathan finally began to calm under her gentle strokes, his sobs quieting as he clung to her.

Ethan's gaze swept the room—sharp, assessing, alert. He

stepped inside, then stopped abruptly, every muscle coiled tight, ready to protect.

A floorboard creaked from somewhere down the hallway.

Sienna's breath caught. Every nerve in her body went rigid. She stared at Ethan, barely able to breathe. "There's someone in the house."

FOUR

Ethan moved swiftly into the shadowed hallway, gun in hand—the one he'd grabbed from the top drawer as he bolted from his room at the sound of Nathan's scream. Ethan's chest burned from the adrenaline surge, his breath tight, ears straining for any sound beyond the pounding of his pulse.

He glanced back into the guest room.

Sienna was on her knees on the bed, clutching Nathan close. Her voice quavered as she prayed, her face as stricken as their son's. Nathan clung to her, silent now but shaking.

"Lock the door." His voice came out low, sharp.

Sienna sprang from the bed as he pulled the door shut. The soft click of the lock resonated like a hammer strike in the silence.

Ethan moved through the house, every sense on high alert, the air charged with tension. The hallway stretched before him, shadows hugging the corners. The familiar scent of wood polish and old pine lingered in the air. He couldn't hear any movement beyond the whisper of his footsteps. Just a heavy, unnatural stillness that made the hairs on the back of his neck stand on end.

The floor was cool beneath his bare feet as he moved down the hallway, each step measured, his Glock steady in his grip. A sliver of moonlight filtered through the living room window, casting long shadows across the floorboards. Every creak of the old house was deafening. He kept his back to the wall, sweeping the muzzle ahead as he cleared each room.

The living room was empty. So was the kitchen. Nothing out of place.

But the silence was thick, like the house itself was holding its breath.

His muscles coiled tighter with every step as he turned the corner toward the mudroom, pulse thudding in his ears.

A flicker of movement snagged the edge of his vision.

He surged forward, adrenaline spiking, just in time to see a dark figure slip out through the mudroom window. Ethan crossed the room in three swift strides and yanked open the exterior door, setting off the house alarm. Cold night air rushed in as his gaze swept the yard. He caught a glimpse of the intruder's black-clad form disappearing beyond the porch spotlight, vanishing into the trees.

Ethan canceled the alarm, then stepped onto the porch, scanning the darkness. Chasing the intruder now would be pointless. Whoever it was had too much of a lead.

He lowered the gun, frustration knotting in his gut. His breath fogged faintly in the cool air as he stepped back inside and approached the window. He noticed the pane had been removed cleanly. That's how the intruder had gotten in—without tripping the alarm or forcing the locks.

A chill slid down his spine.

Someone had been inside his home. The place where Sienna and Nathan were supposed to be safe.

His fingers flexed around the Glock, unspent adrenaline still coursing through his veins. He'd promised to protect them, and he'd already failed.

Jaw set, he backed away from the window and went into the kitchen, where he'd left his phone charging on the counter. Ideally, he would've tucked the Glock into the waistband of his pajama pants, but they weren't designed to hold a firearm.

Especially not a loaded one. The thing would sag, shift or fall straight down his leg. Not exactly the kind of accident he needed right now.

Carter picked up on the fifth ring, voice rough with sleep. "Sheriff?"

Guilt flashed through him for waking his deputy. But this couldn't wait. He pulled out a drawer and locked the Glock away. "I need a secure location for Sienna and Nathan. Off-grid. No questions. Can you make that happen?"

A pause. Then the rustle of sheets and Carter clearing his throat. "There's the Reynolds' place. Old hunting cabin up near Elk Ridge. No cell signal. No neighbors for miles."

Ethan scrubbed a hand over the back of his neck, unease coiling tight beneath his skin. "Is it stocked?"

"Last I checked, yeah. I'll call ahead at first light, make sure it's ready."

"Good." Ethan paced the length of the kitchen into the mud-room, each step dragging tension through his limbs. "Don't tell anyone where we'll be. Not even the team."

"You got it. What's going on, Ethan?"

He paused, crossing one arm over his T-shirt-covered chest and propping the other on top, phone pressed to his ear. "I'll explain later. Just let me know if the Reynolds' place is a go."

"I'm on it. You need backup?"

"Not yet." His gaze shifted in the direction of the hallway. Sienna and Nathan were behind a locked door at the end of the hall. He needed to check on them, make sure they were safe. "I'll let you know. We just need to change location."

"Copy that. I'll take care of it."

Ethan pinched the bridge of his nose, a dull ache spreading behind his eyes as the adrenaline wore off. "Any news on the semi?"

"Nothing yet."

His breath hissed between his teeth. "Semitrucks don't just vanish."

"This one did." He could almost hear Carter's shrug.

"Not possible, Carter. Dig deeper." He stared at the dark trees beyond the glassless window. Was the intruder still out there? Lying in wait beyond the trees for Ethan to let down his guard?

"I intend to."

"And—"

"I know. Keep you posted."

"I need to know if the semi malfunctioned or came at us deliberately." The image of that massive rig bearing down on them—of Sienna's panicked gasps and Nathan's cries—flashed behind his eyes.

"It probably malfunctioned."

His grip tightened on the phone. "I want facts, Carter, not guesswork."

"Sure thing, boss. I'll keep investigating."

"Thanks." Ethan ended the call and stood still, every muscle wired as he listened for anything out of place. Nathan's terrified scream resounded in his mind—along with the chilling thought of what might've happened if his son hadn't woken when he did.

Was that divine intervention?

Ethan didn't know. But right now, he was grateful that someone's prayer had been heard.

He reset the alarm. He needed to board the window. But first he wanted to check on Sienna and Nathan. He turned and headed toward the hall.

They were counting on him.

And this time, he wouldn't fail them.

After locking the door, Sienna crouched beside the bed, trying to project calm for Nathan's sake. Her son was still trembling, his eyes wide with the kind of fear no child should ever have to know.

"Hey, peanut." She stroked his dark hair, keeping her voice light and steady. "I need you to be brave for Mommy, okay?"

He nodded, lips quivering.

She lifted him off the bed and placed him on the floor. His little blue police pajamas were rumpled from sleep, one leg rucked up to below the knee. She gently tugged it down. "You know, police are very brave."

Nathan nodded. "Like Sheriff Callahan."

Her chest squeezed. "Yes, just like him." She traced the printed badge on his chest. "And you're very brave, aren't you?"

"I scared the bad man away."

He was so much like his father it hurt. Not just his eyes and handsome features, but even at this tender age, he had an instinct to protect.

"Yes, you did, and I'm so proud of you." Something about Nathan's puffed out chest in his little police pj's forced a lump to her throat. "Come with me." She closed his little hand in hers. "You're a very good hider. When we play hide-and-go-seek, you always find the best hiding places. I want you to pretend we're playing, and I need to come find you. Can you do that?"

Nathan nodded.

"Good." She led him to the closet. "Hide in here."

Nathan stepped inside and crouched down.

"Good boy." Sienna hurried back to the bed to collect the pillows, and that's when she noticed the cushion on the floor beside the bed. A shiver ran through her entire frame. Had the intruder taken it from the chair beneath the window and dropped it there? Was she looking at her intended murder weapon? Shaking off the panic threatening to consume her, she grabbed the pillows and knelt in the closet doorway. "I'm going to stack these in front of you like a wall. Stay behind them, just like we practiced when we play secret hideout. Can you do that for Mommy?"

Nathan nodded again, his small hands shaking as he helped her stack the pillows.

"And be super quiet," she whispered, pressing her index finger to her mouth.

He copied her, mimicking the gesture with solemn eyes.

She gave her sweet little boy a reassuring smile, even as her heart cracked for him.

Once he was settled, she quietly closed the closet door, then scanned the room. She needed a weapon. If something went wrong and Ethan… She couldn't go there. But she wasn't going to sit by and wait, either. She'd do everything in her power to protect her child. Her gaze landed on the earth-tone ceramic lamp on the nightstand—sturdy, heavy, just the right size to swing if she had to. She yanked the cord free and gripped the cool base with both hands. Not ideal, but better than a cushion or a pillow—which were her only other options.

She flattened herself to the wall beside the door, lamp raised, breath locked in her chest as she strained to catch the faintest sound from the hall. If it wasn't Ethan, she'd be ready.

Moments later, a faint creak echoed from somewhere down the hall.

Sienna tensed, lamp raised higher, breath locked in her throat. She angled her body, ready to strike if the door so much as moved.

Another step. Closer.

Please, God, let it be Ethan.

Then a soft knock. "Sienna? It's me."

Relief slammed into her, buckling her knees. She exhaled the breath she'd been holding, the heavy lamp trembling in her grip. She hugged the lamp close with one hand, then hurried to unlock the door.

Ethan stepped into the room. He clasped her shoulders gently. His eyes searched her face, swept over her pink pajamas as if assessing her for injury. "Are you okay?"

Her voice caught in the tight knot of her chest. She cleared her throat. "We're okay."

He scanned the room. "Where's Nathan?"

"Hiding." She crossed to the closet and opened the door. Nathan sat where she'd left him, hidden behind the pillow wall.

He blinked up at her, his lower lip trembling. The moment he saw Ethan behind her, he scrambled out of the closet.

Ethan dropped to one knee, arms open. "Hey, buddy. You okay?"

Nathan launched himself into his arms.

Ethan caught him, wrapping him in a solid, reassuring hug. "You did good. Real good. I'm proud of you."

Nathan nodded against his shoulder, clinging to him.

Sienna's grip on the lamp loosened. Her arm ached. Her chest ached. She lowered the lamp to the floor and sank onto the bed, exhaustion crashing over her like a wave.

She watched Ethan cradle their son, his hand protective against Nathan's back, and a tight knot of emotion twisted inside her.

Until tonight, he hadn't known Nathan existed, and in that moment, no one would have guessed it. He met her gaze, his eyes steady, penetrating—like his world had shifted. The quiet, unspoken tension in his expression undid her.

A knot, hot and aching, rose in her throat. She blinked hard, the sting behind her eyes giving her away.

Nathan had no idea Ethan was his father, but he seemed to instinctively know he was safe in his arms.

"Hey, buddy. I need to speak with your mom. Do you think it'd be all right if I put you back to bed?"

Nathan shook his head vigorously against Ethan's muscular shoulder. "No, I'm scared if the bad man comes back. I want to sleep in your bed."

Sienna's heart clenched. Her brave little boy was trying to put big feelings into small words.

She expected Ethan to hesitate, maybe even glance her way for guidance. But he didn't.

Instead, his arms tightened around Nathan, and his voice came out a little huskier than normal. "All right. Then that's exactly where you'll sleep."

Sienna blinked. The quiet certainty in Ethan's tone wrapped around her like a blanket. He didn't look overwhelmed or unsure. He looked like a man who'd just stepped into a role he was made for.

She swallowed hard, emotions tightening her throat—mostly guilt for all the years Ethan had lost as a father. He hadn't known he was a parent. And yet here he was, this strong, steady presence her son was clinging to like a lifeline.

Ethan stood, Nathan tucked against him, his protective hand still cradling his son's back. He met her gaze over Nathan's shoulder. Something unspoken passed between them—something she couldn't name, but it made her chest ache.

He tore his gaze away, turning his attention back to Nathan. "You okay to walk?" He brushed a hand gently over Nathan's back.

Nathan nodded but made no move to release the stranglehold he had on Ethan.

Ethan's mouth curved faintly. "Guess not."

He adjusted his hold and turned toward the door. Sienna followed, her limbs heavy. Her eyes stung, but she blinked the tears back. There'd be time to cry later.

They just had to make it through tonight.

Ethan carried Nathan down the hall, his strides long. Sienna kept up, her gaze catching on how brightly the house was lit. Ethan must've turned on every light. She watched the way her son clung to him like it was something he did all the time, his slight frame curling closer, his small fingers fisting the fabric of Ethan's white T-shirt. As if his little heart already knew this man was his safe place.

Ethan nudged the bedroom door open with his foot and stepped inside. The room was dim, quiet. A single lamp cast a warm pool of light across the rumpled covers on one side of the bed. The other side was undisturbed. Sienna's gaze lingered there. So different from how she slept—sprawled in the middle, claiming all the space, unless Nathan crawled in beside her.

Sienna rushed forward to pull back the untouched side of the bed so Ethan could ease their son down onto the mattress. He did so like he was afraid Nathan might break. Together, they adjusted the covers, tucking them around Nathan.

"You're safe here." Ethan carefully stroked a hand over his son's hair, his voice quiet.

Nathan curled on his side and pulled the covers up to his chin. His thumb slipped into his mouth, and Sienna's heart pinched. He hadn't done that in ages.

Ethan adjusted the blanket one more time, then glanced at her.

She brushed a knuckle down Nathan's cheek. "You want me to stay with you a little while?"

He shook his head, his eyes drooping. "I got the sheriff."

That tiny broken whisper undid her. She blinked rapidly. Ethan was never going to forgive her for keeping Nathan a secret. She knew this and had accepted it. She just hadn't considered until now that Nathan would one day hold her sins against her, too.

She cleared her throat and managed to whisper, "Okay, baby."

She stepped back, her gaze meeting Ethan's over their son's sleepy form. He didn't speak, just gave a slight nod. Something flickered between them, a connection time hadn't erased. It should have given her hope, but she knew better than to let herself believe in second chances or redemption. Not when the past still stood between them like a wall neither had the tools to tear down.

Nathan fell asleep almost immediately and Ethan followed her out, leaving the door open. "Just in case he calls out." He dragged a hand through his hair, looked back at the partially open door. "Is he going to be okay?"

Sienna folded her arms, not to protect herself against him but to hold herself together. She fell into step beside him. "I don't know. He's seen a lot in the past few days. That's not something he'll quickly forget."

Ethan's voice was quiet. "Did he witness you being shot?"

She shook her head, a strand of hair brushing her cheek. "No, but he saw the man chasing me." She swallowed hard, the copper tang of fear still clinging to the back of her throat. "He'd been waiting for me in the car. I'd popped into the stables to collect the jacket I'd forgotten after working with a stallion earlier in the day…and that's when I overheard Trip with the man."

Ethan exhaled, dragging his hands down his face, the rasp of stubble loud in the predawn hush. "The intruder escaped. He got in by removing the windowpane in the mudroom and slipped out the same way."

Sienna shivered. The thought of a stranger getting in so quietly made her never want to sleep again. She rubbed her arms, trying to chase away the lingering chill that had settled in her bones. "Did you get a look at him?"

His brow twitched, then he gave a short shake of his head. "Dressed in black. Balaclava. Gloves. I saw nothing identifiable."

She wrapped her arms tighter around herself. "Do you think it was the same man from the stables?"

"If I had to guess, I'd say yes."

"How did he know where to find us?" she whispered.

Ethan scratched his jaw, his other hand braced on his lean hip. "Either he followed you—" he leaned back against the wall "—or the bloodline fraud you uncovered at your father's ranch is tied to the one Trip was involved in." Ethan raised a brow, his gaze steady. "Someone who knows you're here might've tipped him off."

Her stomach knotted, a tight, hot twist of dread.

"What if he comes back?" That thought alone was enough to give her palpitations.

Ethan stood motionless, the tension in his frame barely leashed. "I'm arranging a secure location to take you and Nathan. As soon as I hear from Carter, we'll head off."

"What about you?" She looked down, hoping he wouldn't read how scared she was. How much she needed him.

He tipped her chin with the lightest touch of his finger. His eyes locked with hers—steady, unreadable. "I promised to protect you and Nathan. I have no intention of breaking that promise."

She believed him. Ethan wasn't the kind of man to break a promise. But was this about duty or something more?

A part of her—a foolish, hopeful part—ached to believe it was personal. That maybe, just maybe, he was starting to forgive her. That he wanted to be Nathan's father.

But how could she believe that when she didn't know if he was putting his life on the line because he still cared…or simply because he wore the badge and saw this as nothing more than his job?

FIVE

The last nail sank with a solid thunk beneath Ethan's hammer. He stepped back from the window in the mudroom, surveying the makeshift plywood barrier. It wasn't pretty, but it would hold. Not a permanent fix, but enough to keep the house secure until he replaced the glass.

He returned the hammer to the shelf and rubbed the back of his neck. He'd boarded the hole, checked every door and window—twice. Still, unease clawed at his gut.

Who was after Sienna? She'd left all those years ago to protect him from a threat. Now she was back, running from a threat of her own, which could make their son a target, too.

Exhausted but wired, Ethan stepped out onto the porch. The chill of the early May morning wrapped him in its cool freshness, seeping through his thermal shirt, raising goose bumps along his arms. He let the quiet settle around him. The sky hovered in that brief pocket of time before sunrise, too light to be night, too dark to be day.

Everything was too still.

The boards creaked under his boots as he crossed to the railing and braced his hands against the wood. He drew in a deep breath, then released it in a slow stream, watching his breath curl into the air and vanish.

Sienna had known about the bloodline fraud and had kept it to herself. Why? If she couldn't come to him, she could have gone to the police, a federal agent. Had she really been trying to protect him, or was there more to the story than she was letting on?

Was she telling him the whole truth? Or had she been involved back then?

The thought turned his stomach. What about Idaho? Could he trust her version of events? Could he trust *her*? He had no evidence she wasn't part of the fraud—only her word. And after the way she'd left, that didn't count for much.

She might be lying to save herself.

But…

Nathan looked too much like him to be anyone else's child. *His son.*

He was a father.

Even hours after Sienna had walked into his office with Nathan, the revelation was still sinking in.

The weight of that discovery pressed heavy on his chest. He could still feel Nathan's arms around his neck, the faint tremors in his small body as he'd clung to him, the hero worship in his blue eyes when he'd run from his hiding place into Ethan's arms. He couldn't describe the surge of powerful emotions that had slammed into him. The love, the fierce need to protect.

He ran a hand over his face and exhaled an uneven breath. Was this what it felt like to be a father? That punch of emotion when someone so small trusted you to fix everything? This bone-deep ache to shield, to fight if he had to?

His heart still pinched at Nathan's whispered words: *I got the sheriff.* Like trusting him was second nature.

Like Ethan had been there all along.

But he hadn't.

Five years. He'd missed everything. The good, the bad, the firsts. All of it.

And now he was supposed to step into a role as father to a child he'd just met. A protector to a woman who had once broken his heart. A woman who still had a claim on it, whether he wanted to admit that or not.

He lifted his eyes to the horizon. A thin ribbon of gold edged over the eastern ridge, chasing shadows from the pines.

"I don't know what You want from me." His voice came out rough, even though it was just above a whisper. "Did You send her back to me…or just for me to protect her?"

The silence gave no answer. Only the wind stirred, brushing through the trees, bringing the sharp tang of pine from the ridge.

He hadn't expected a response. It had been a long time since he'd prayed with any real conviction. Even longer since he believed God might actually be listening.

Behind him, the door creaked open.

He turned.

Sienna stepped onto the porch, her boots tapping against the quiet morning. Wrapped in a thick blanket over her pajamas, her hair in a messy ponytail with tendrils framing her pretty face, she looked at him with shadows in her hazel eyes. The blanket dwarfed her slender frame, but it didn't hide the caution in her movements.

His heart gave an uncomfortable jolt.

She held up a mug, offering him a tentative smile. "Thought you could use this."

He didn't want her to smile at him. He didn't want to feel a single thing. But he did. He felt a whole lot. And none of it brought him the peace he used to value more than anything.

Sienna stepped up beside him and handed him one of the steaming mugs. Their fingers brushed—brief, accidental. A spark he hadn't expected zipped up his arm.

He curled his fingers tighter around the mug and looked away, willing his pulse to settle. He shouldn't have felt anything, but he did. Maybe it was just the cold. Or maybe it was the reminder that, like it or not, his heart hadn't let go.

"Thanks." He cupped the mug between his hands, inhaling

the rich aroma of freshly brewed coffee, and let the warmth soak into his fingers.

She drew the blanket tighter around her shoulders with one hand and leaned her hip against the railing beside him. "It's cold."

"It usually is just before dawn." His gaze swept the horizon beyond the field to where the tall pines stood silhouetted against the fading stars.

"Yes, I remember." Her voice was soft, barely a whisper.

He didn't look at her. He couldn't.

If he did, he might forget how angry he was supposed to be.

But no matter how complicated things were between them, he wasn't going to walk away—not now. Not when his son needed him.

They stood in silence, sipping coffee, while the first light of daybreak began to paint soft hues across the sky. In the distance, the dawn chorus began—gentle birdsong rising from the trees like a hymn to the new day. The scent of dew-drenched grass and pine drifted on the crisp morning air, fresh and earthy. Sienna closed her eyes for a moment, breathing it in. A new day. They were alive. And for that alone, she was grateful.

She glanced at Ethan from beneath her lashes. His jaw was clenched, the muscle ticking beneath his skin as he stared out at the horizon. His shoulders held tension, but it wasn't the kind that came from fatigue. This was deeper—coiled energy barely held in check.

He looked tired. Not just physically, but in a way that stabbed at her heart. Like he was carrying more than she could ever imagine.

Dark stubble covered his chiseled jawline, making him look rugged and right off the front cover of a men's style and grooming magazine all at once. He had a faint scar near his temple that hadn't been there six years ago.

The man beside her was both familiar and changed. And despite everything, her heart ached at the sight of him. She'd unintentionally caused him so much pain. A pain she carried, too.

He would never know she still loved him. Always had. Always would.

Once, he'd been her everything—her best friend, her safe place, the man who held her heart in ways no one else ever could.

How could she not love him?

He'd given her Nathan. And every time she looked at their son—so much like his father it stole her breath—she was reminded of everything she'd lost.

She breathed in the rich scent of coffee, rising with the steam from her mug. Ethan had been so funny, so effortlessly charming in a way that had made her fall harder and faster than she ever meant to.

They'd been carefree. Full of plans for a future—simple dreams: marriage, a porch swing, a houseful of kids and a dog.

A future they'd never have now.

For I know the plans I have for you. The words from her favorite scripture in Jeremiah came to mind. *Plans to prosper you and not to harm you, plans to give you hope and a future.*

Once she'd clung to that truth. Now she couldn't picture what it might look like.

In the quiet moments, she sometimes scrolled through photos from the past. Pictures of her and Ethan when they were happy. She'd pause on the ones where he smiled at her like she was the only woman in the world.

Just remembering now made her throat tighten.

She missed his contagious laugh. His steady presence. The way he made her feel safe—like nothing could ever touch her when she was with him.

She missed him with a longing that never really left.

But some things were better left unsaid. For both their sakes.

She turned her eyes to the sky, heart aching.

Lord, if this is part of Your plan...show me what to do with it.

The silence between her and Ethan began to stretch her nerves. When he shifted, she spoke. "What happens now?"

He glanced at her, brow furrowed. "We wait for Carter's call."

She nodded slowly, wishing she knew how to get past the wall Ethan had erected between them. "The secure location?"

He nodded. "A cabin in Elk Ridge. Off-grid but secure."

The thought of packing up Nathan again, of putting her little boy through more upheaval, twisted her stomach. "How much longer do you think we'll be running?"

Ethan looked out across the ridge, his jaw set. "We aren't running, Sienna. We're changing location for your and Nathan's safety. Whoever is after you knows you're here, which means you aren't safe."

A beat of silence passed before she said quietly, "You could make it safe."

"Eventually." He kept his attention on the horizon. "But that would take too long." He finally met her gaze. "We'll find whoever is behind this. You have my word."

She stared into the eyes of the man she'd once trusted with her whole heart. Part of her still did. "I believe you."

He gave a firm, single nod, as if to say, *Good, the matter is settled.*

There was so much more she wanted to say but opted for "Thank you." She buried her nose in her mug. "For going above and beyond for us."

She felt his gaze on her. "You don't have to thank me for protecting our son."

The words lingered between them. Their son. Their past. The fragile thread of a future.

She nodded, swallowing the emotion rising in her throat. "I

know you might never forgive me, Ethan. But I'll do everything in my power to earn your forgiveness."

His voice, when he spoke, was low and firm. "What I don't understand is why you kept the bloodline fraud to yourself."

She stilled, her breath catching. Of all the things he could've asked, she'd braced for that one the least.

Sienna lowered her mug, her fingers tightening around the ceramic. "Because I didn't know who I could trust." She pressed her lips together, then looked out at the faint glow edging the horizon. "And I was scared."

He said nothing, but she could feel the weight of his stare pressing on her. Did he think she was involved? How could he think she would ever be part of something like that?

She turned to him. Her voice trembled as she spoke. "I saw something I wasn't supposed to see. Enough to know people were covering it up. Powerful people. I wanted to go to the authorities. I *tried*, but then I got that message."

"The threat on my life." His tone was flat, almost bored.

She bit her lip, hurt. She knew he held her leaving against her, but she never considered that he might not trust her. "They said if I didn't disappear, you'd die. I couldn't take that risk. And when I discovered I was pregnant..." She blinked rapidly, hating the weak tears. Yet she couldn't say whether they were from memories of the past or because Ethan thought so little of her. "I didn't just have me to protect anymore. I had Nathan, too."

Pain flickered in Ethan's eyes. "You could've come to me. Trusted me, Sienna."

"I wanted to," she whispered, barely holding it together. "More than anything. But how could I take the chance? You were a deputy. I didn't know how deep it went. I didn't know if someone in your department was involved. I didn't know if *you* were part of it."

He flinched like she'd slapped him but he didn't speak, and that silence was louder than anything he could have said.

Her voice cracked. "I'm sorry. I hated myself for even thinking it. But I was terrified. When they hurt you, I thought you might die. How could I make you a target again?" She blinked against the rising sting behind her eyes. "So I left. I made the choice I thought I had. A horrible one…but at the time, it felt like the only way to keep you alive." She risked a glance at him. "I've carried that fear every day since. The guilt. The regret. Leaving you…it wrecked me, Ethan. But losing you would've destroyed me."

His jaw clenched. He looked away, out across the land that rolled quiet and cold beneath the breaking dawn.

Emotion clogged her throat. She dropped her gaze, afraid to see judgment in his expression. "I'm sorry I left. I'm sorry I kept Nathan away. I've lived with the guilt for years. Every birthday Nathan had without you, every time he asked if he had a daddy like the other kids. I never stopped regretting what I did…but I *did* what I thought would keep you alive."

His chest rose and fell with a long, silent breath. He studied his coffee as if the answers might be there. "You should've told me anyway," he said at last.

She nodded slowly, her voice catching. "I know."

Ethan shifted his weight, his boots scraping the porch. "So why did you come back?"

"I can't do this alone. I can't protect Nathan on my own. I need your help."

"And then?"

She brushed away a strand of hair that blew across her mouth. "I don't know."

"When this is all over, Sienna," he clarified. "Are you going to take my son and leave Hope Haven?"

"I don't know." She wished her voice was stronger, that she was more decisive.

With a frustrated growl, Ethan tossed the rest of his coffee across the dew-covered grass. He faced her fully, his eyes harder than she'd ever seen them.

"That would be over my dead body." He turned his back, throwing over his shoulder, "Before bed last night, you asked about doing your laundry. I suggest you get it done, because we're leaving in a couple of hours." His boots clomped loudly as he stomped back into the house.

Ethan shoved open the mudroom door with more force than necessary, the slam echoing in the quiet house. The screen door banged shut behind him, but the hollow thud didn't quiet the echo of his sharp words. *Over my dead body.*

The thought of Sienna leaving again—of losing Nathan for a second time—ignited something raw and primal inside him. Something he didn't know how to control. He dragged a hand through his hair, frustration sparking beneath his skin. Better anger than fear. At least anger didn't make him feel helpless.

He stomped through the mudroom, every muscle tight, every thought clouded with fury. His boots boomed across the hardwood as he moved into the kitchen.

She didn't know if she'd stay?

He tossed his empty mug into the sink with a loud clatter and gripped the edge of the counter, shoulders rising and falling with uneven breaths. He needed to cool down. Think.

But he couldn't.

His phone buzzed in his back pocket. He snatched it out, glared at the screen.

Carter. *Finally.*

He swiped to answer. "Go ahead."

"Hey, Ethan, the Reynolds' cabin is good to go. Stocked and ready. I'll send you the GPS coordinates." Jack sounded tired but alert.

Relief loosened something in Ethan's chest. He let out a breath, nodding to no one. That was one thing sorted.

"Appreciate it."

"There's something else." Carter's voice held a weight that caught Ethan's attention. The shift in the deputy's tone drew Ethan's brows together.

"Yeah?" He put his phone on speaker, set it on the counter and turned on the tap to rinse his coffee mug.

"We traced the semi. It was a rental through a shell company in Billings. But get this. The payment came from an account in the name of Jacob Blake."

Ethan froze. The name landed like a gut punch. Cold prickled across his scalp.

He straightened slowly, braced one hand on the sink. "That's not possible. Jacob's been dead for a year."

"I know." Carter blew out a breath, and Ethan heard rustling paper. "But the bank confirmed it. ID matches. Signature too."

A whisper of movement behind him made Ethan glance over his shoulder.

Sienna stood frozen in the doorway between the kitchen and the mudroom, her hands white-knuckled around her coffee mug, her face drained of all color, lips parted in a shocked O.

He met her eyes.

She slowly shook her head as if she were coming out of a fog. "How?"

He didn't know, but if Jacob Blake was behind this from beyond the grave, Ethan was going to find out.

SIX

Sienna eased the soft cotton T-shirt over Nathan's head, help-ing him to push his arms through the sleeves with practiced care, though her thoughts were a thousand miles away.

Jack Carter's words still rang in her ears: *But get this. The payment came from an account in the name of Jacob Blake.*

The shock of hearing that still vibrated through her. It was hard to reconcile the man she knew as a child with the man it seemed her father really was. He'd once been a steady, ground-ing presence. He'd taught her how to ride a horse before she could even reach the stirrups. Taught her how to fish. How to braid rope. How to find the North Star and never lose her way.

Now she was supposed to believe that he hired a semitruck from beyond the grave to run them off the road?

"Are we going on a 'venture, Mommy?" Nathan's sleepy voice tugged her back to the present as she buttoned his jeans. He blinked up at her, his dark hair a soft halo around his face and Woody, his favorite toy, clutched tight in one hand.

She nodded, forcing an easy smile. "Yes, peanut." She gently brushed her fingers over his hair. "We are."

He beamed up at her. "Can I wear my Woody boots? I want to be a sheriff today."

Sienna managed a small smile. "Of course. But let's get your socks first."

She reached into his bag and pulled out a pair of rolled-up

Toy Story socks. She sat him on the bed and handed him one so he could help with the task of pulling them on. Then she helped him into his boots.

Her father hadn't been a saint—she'd seen the proof. He was involved in the bloodline fraud. She couldn't pretend otherwise. Not after finding the falsified breeding records. Not when he hadn't denied it when she asked him about his involvement outright. And he told her to forget what she saw. That it was bigger than both of them, and she needed to keep her mouth shut about what she thought she knew. Or bring down more trouble than she could ever imagine.

They were close when she was little, but by her mid-teens, he had become distant. Was that when it started? When he'd gotten tangled in the fraud? He hadn't just shut her out—he'd changed. Became cold. Secretive. Angry sometimes. She'd blamed herself, but now…now she wondered if he'd been trying to protect her all along. Keeping her at arm's length so she wouldn't be dragged down with him.

Nathan wiggled, trying to escape her grip, and she forced herself to refocus. She brushed his hair back from his forehead, then zipped his hoodie and handed him his toast.

From the window, she caught a glimpse of Ethan moving across the gravel drive, his tall frame silhouetted by the rising sun. Like her, he'd showered and changed since Jack called. He wore a tan T-shirt, a brown flannel shirt left open at the front and dark jeans. A large duffel was slung over one shoulder as he headed to his patrol truck. Every move was precise and efficient. He hadn't said much after Jack's call. Just told her to be ready to leave ASAP.

She zipped Nathan's bag and placed it next to hers near the bedroom door.

It still hurt that she hadn't been there when her dad died. By the time she found out—just days later—he'd already been buried.

She may not have witnessed his body being lowered into the earth, but she knew in her heart he was dead. Someone was using his name and accounts to cover their tracks. And she was going to prove it.

Because whoever was behind this wasn't just trying to erase the truth. They were trying to erase *her*.

And she wasn't about to let that happen.

Ethan adjusted the duffel strap on his shoulder and gave the perimeter one more sweep with his gaze. Nothing but trees, fence posts and the long Montana horizon. Still, his gut wouldn't unclench.

The sky was pale with the early sun, crisp and cloudless. The kind of morning that promised a pleasant day.

Somewhere in the distance, a hawk cried—a sharp, solitary note that echoed from above.

Carter's voice played on a loop in his head: *The payment came from an account in Jacob Blake's name.*

Jacob Blake. A dead man. A man who had once hauled him out of a frozen creek when his horse spooked. Who had given him his blessing to marry his daughter. Ethan had never trusted him completely, had suspected his business dealings weren't always above board. But he'd never pegged Jacob for someone who'd try to kill his own child.

On the porch, waiting to be packed into the truck, was food, first aid, extra ammo, cold weather gear. Everything they'd need if they had to stay off-grid for a few days. Or longer.

The sound of the door opening pulled Ethan's attention back to the house.

Sienna stepped onto the porch, a carry-on in each hand. Nathan trailed at her side with his small backpack bouncing against his back, his boots clomping on the boards. Woody dangled from one hand.

Ethan started toward them, meeting them halfway. "I'll get those." He reached for the bags.

She handed them over without protest, then crouched to help Nathan take off his backpack.

Nathan hurried ahead of her but caught the toe of his boot and stumbled forward.

"Whoa there, partner." Ethan grabbed Nathan before he fell and steadied him on his feet. "Sheriffs don't go down easy." He ruffled Nathan's hair.

Nathan beamed up at him. "Yes, sir."

"Do you need help with this?" Sienna glanced down at the supplies he'd gathered on the porch to take with them.

"No, I've got it." He put down the bags, slipping his duffle off his shoulder and setting it on the porch beside Sienna and Nathan. "Probably best to get the supplies in the truck first, then load the bags."

Sienna nodded. "I'll get Nathan into his seat."

As she crossed the porch with Nathan beside her, Ethan turned back to the truck and caught a glint of silver beneath the chassis. At first, he thought it might be a bit of moisture catching the morning light, but something about the way it reflected the light wasn't right.

"Sienna, wait."

She paused on the steps. "What is it?"

"Just wait here." He moved closer to his truck, lowering himself to one knee as his gaze swept under the frame near the rear wheel. A wire, taped in place, caught his attention. It ran along the undercarriage, leading to a small black box nestled beside the fuel tank. The dirt around it had been disturbed, brushed over clumsily like someone had tried to hide what they had done but didn't care enough to do a good job.

The breath left his lungs in a sharp, silent exhale.

It was a bomb.

Ethan's chest tightened so suddenly it stole his breath. Every instinct sharpened at once. His pulse surged, his skin prickled and his limbs locked with the kind of stillness that came from sheer survival training.

Sienna and Nathan were steps from the truck.

For a heartbeat, he couldn't move. Couldn't think.

He had always been the one to act, to protect, to take charge when everything around him fell apart. But in that moment, facing the very real possibility of losing Sienna and the son he'd only just discovered, Ethan found himself completely out of his depth.

His lips parted, and a single thought rose above the roar of panic.

God, please.

The prayer formed without prompting, born from the deepest place inside him. He hadn't spoken a real prayer in years, not since he finally realized that God wasn't answering his prayers to bring Sienna back to him.

But now, with her and Nathan steps from death, Ethan knew he couldn't carry this alone.

He glanced to the sky. "I know I don't have the right to ask, but I'm asking anyway. Not for me. For them. Please don't let them die."

A verse came to him, not fully remembered, but enough to wrap around his heart like an anchor in the storm.

God is our refuge and strength, a very present help in trouble.

He didn't know where it came from. Maybe from church as a boy. Maybe from his mother's soft voice when she would quote scriptures.

But the words steadied him.

He raised a hand toward Sienna, who had taken a few curious steps forward.

"Sienna, don't come any closer. It's a bomb."

She gasped, confusion knitting her expression. "A what?"

He knew she'd heard him, so he didn't repeat himself. "Take Nathan and get as far away from the truck as you can."

She looked at him for the space of a breath, and then he saw it. She recognized the gravity in his face, the sharp edge of something more than worry.

"Ethan—"

"I'm right behind you."

Without delay, she scooped Nathan into her arms and ran for the side of the house.

Ethan moved, positioning himself between them and the truck.

They had just reached the corner of the house when an explosion erupted behind them, hurling a shockwave through the air as the patrol truck detonated in a blinding burst of light and smoke. The blast slammed into him with a heat so intense it stole the breath from his lungs. They hit the ground hard, Ethan shielding Sienna and Nathan with his body as the explosion ripped through the truck. The impact shook the earth beneath them, a brutal roar followed by a rain of heat and debris.

Sienna screamed his name.

Nathan's petrified sobs tore at his heart.

The world crackled and hissed around them, the scorched air thick with smoke and the acrid tang of burning fuel. Ethan stayed down, arms braced over Sienna and Nathan, listening— waiting—for a second blast that didn't come.

When it was clear the worst had passed, he shifted his weight just enough to check them, mindful of any sharp debris.

Sienna lay half beneath him, curled protectively around their son. Her eyes locked with his, wide and shocked, her face streaked with soot. Nathan whimpered in her arms, his little hands clinging to her jacket, his face buried in her shoulder.

"Ethan…"

His ears rang from the blast, a high-pitched hum that refused to fade. The heat still radiated across his back, and the acrid bite of burning fuel clawed at his throat. "Are you hurt?"

Wide-eyed, she shook her head. Her lips moved, but it took her a moment to find her voice. "We're…" She ran a hand over Nathan, relief whooshing her breath from her lungs. "We're okay."

They were okay.

They were alive.

The surge of his own relief was almost overwhelming. He closed his eyes for a heartbeat, grounding himself in the feel of her beneath his hands, in the sound of Nathan's breaths, in the certainty that they were still here.

Adrenaline pulsed through his veins, but now it was mixed with something else. The memory of the prayer he'd whispered only moments before the blast.

Please don't let them die.

The words circled back now with quiet power. It had been years since he'd prayed, and even as the words left his mouth, he hadn't expected to be heard.

Yet… He couldn't explain it.

He didn't know if it was coincidence or grace, but the echo in his heart was impossible to ignore. The moment he asked—the moment he surrendered—help had come. Not in the form of angels or miracles, but in a split-second choice. A warning. A chance to get them out.

His hand smoothed over Nathan's back, and he exhaled slowly. God had answered his prayer! "Thank You, Lord."

He got up, then helped Sienna, who was still clutching Nathan, to her feet. Ethan turned back to the mangled remains of his patrol truck. The fire crackled angrily, thick black smoke billowing into the air. Flames licked the gravel beneath the frame, and the grass on the north side of the drive had already caught fire. The truck was a blackened shell, the fire eating through what was left of the frame. Any trace of evidence was likely burning with it.

Ethan looked at Sienna and Nathan. She met his gaze, her hazel eyes too big in her face, her hands around Nathan trembling.

He brushed a lock of hair from her face, tucked it behind her ear. "Take him inside. I'll call this in."

She nodded. Without hesitation, she turned and hurried with Nathan into the house.

Ethan reached for his phone, his gaze drifting back to the inferno blazing on the drive.

Something told him this was only the beginning.

Sienna stood in the front room, just behind the large window that looked out over the gravel drive and the smoldering wreckage of Ethan's patrol truck. Nathan was curled up on the couch behind her, huddled beneath a throw blanket with Woody still clutched tight in one arm. His eyes had closed, but every so often, his little body twitched as if still bracing for another blast.

Her own legs hadn't stopped trembling. Her ears still rang faintly.

The truck had exploded maybe forty, fifty feet from the house. Far enough that the flames hadn't reached the porch, thank God. But the blast had lit up the drive and left nothing behind but twisted metal and acrid smoke.

Ethan had saved them. She didn't know how he'd moved so fast or stayed so calm. But she could still feel the weight of his body shielding theirs, the heat of the blast rolling over them like a wave. Her heart hadn't stopped racing since.

Through the glass, she watched him cross the scorched edge of the drive with a fire extinguisher in his hands. He moved with efficiency, sweeping low arcs of suppressant across the dry grass at the north side, tamping down every last ember threatening to crawl toward the fields.

She hadn't realized she was holding her breath until she let it go slowly.

His posture was tense. Each movement was sure and controlled. He hadn't changed. Not really. Not where it counted.

He still had that same quiet strength she remembered. The same instinct to protect, to contain chaos, to step in and make everything okay.

When he straightened, he pulled his phone from his back pocket and turned away from the wind, speaking into it with what looked like clipped precision. She couldn't hear his voice, but she knew the stance. Shoulders squared. Chin tilted. He was giving orders. Delegating. Making things happen.

And somehow, watching him now—soot on his shirt, hair damp with sweat, fire extinguisher in hand—something inside her unfurled.

Because no matter how chaotic things became, Ethan Callahan didn't falter.

And maybe—for the first time in a very long time—she didn't have to carry everything herself.

He turned toward the house and disappeared from view.

A moment later, the front door opened, and he stepped inside, shutting the door behind him. He brushed a hand down his flannel shirt, smearing ash across the fabric. His face was grim and soot-stained. But when his blue eyes found hers, her breath stalled.

He wiped his feet. "I called in the fire. Team from Station Two is already on the way. Should be here soon. This is officially a crime scene."

She nodded, unable to unravel the myriad emotions bombarding her. "What happens now?"

He stepped farther inside, his voice low as he glanced at Nathan curled up on the couch. "Carter's already on his way with a team. They'll want statements from both of us."

Her gaze drifted toward the window. "The truck…"

"Nothing left to save." He glanced down, then back at her. "But I stopped the fire from spreading."

She swallowed. Her mouth had gone dry. "I saw."

Ethan's gaze softened. "As soon as they finish here, we're leaving for the cabin in Elk Ridge."

She met his eyes again. "How? Your truck just got blown up, and my car is in the lockup."

"I have my personal SUV in the garage. It's off the radar. No one knows we'll be using it."

Sienna's throat tightened. She wanted to hold herself together, to stay composed, to keep moving forward like she always had. But the truth was, the fear hadn't left her—not entirely. It sat in her chest like a weight, pressing harder with every heartbeat. The smell of smoke was still on her clothes. The image of the explosion still burned behind her eyes.

They were alive, thanks to Ethan.

That fact alone cracked something open.

She crossed the room in a few quick steps and threw her arms around him. The hug was filled with raw emotion and the sheer relief that they were all still breathing.

"Thank you, Ethan. You saved our lives."

He held her just as tightly, one hand sliding up to cradle the back of her head, the other steady between her shoulder blades. His warmth, his strength, the way he exhaled against her hair. Everything about him anchored her.

For the first time in six years, she didn't feel alone.

And then, without warning, the tears came.

Hot, heavy sobs shook her. She pressed her face to his shoulder, the flood of shock and fear and gratitude pouring out all at once. Now that it was safe to feel it, she couldn't stop.

SEVEN

The road stretched like a ribbon through the pines, silent except for the low hum of tires on pavement and the rhythmic thump of rubber over seams in the asphalt. The forest road curved ahead in quiet surrender—all dust, sunlight and miles of green wilderness. The sun was high in the sky, casting shifting patterns of light through the canopy, dappling the hood of the SUV as it ate up the miles to Elk Ridge.

Ethan glanced at Sienna in the passenger seat beside him, her hair damp from the shower she'd rushed through earlier, her gaze fixed on the endless stretch of forest. She'd been quiet since they left the ranch. Ever since she'd unraveled in his arms like a storm breaking.

He hadn't known what to say then. He didn't know what to say now.

And he wasn't sure what scared him more—how completely inadequate he'd felt…or how much he'd wanted to hold her forever.

He adjusted his grip on the wheel and flicked his gaze to the mirror. Nathan was asleep in his booster seat, Woody tucked under his arm. They'd picked up the new seat just before leaving—the old one had gone up with the truck. He didn't let himself dwell on how differently things could've ended.

His prayer had been answered. Part of him wanted to believe that had been God. Part wanted to chalk it up to coincidence.

Luck. But the memory of that scripture came to mind: *God is our refuge and strength, a very present help in trouble.* He'd had to look up the verse—Psalm 46:1.

He rolled his shoulders, easing the knot between them. The adrenaline from the morning had long since faded, leaving behind a strange clarity—the kind that came after surviving something a man shouldn't have, the kind that made him see what actually mattered. He glanced at Sienna again. She was chewing on her lower lip, deep in thought. Her expression was unreadable, but something fragile shimmered beneath the surface. Like she was holding herself together with sheer force of will.

He wanted to reach out a hand and touch her. Ask her what she was thinking. But too much hung in the balance—the fragile truce between them, Nathan's safety, a past they couldn't undo and the part of him that still hadn't forgiven her…but wasn't ready to let her go, either. And, lest he forget, she'd made it clear she might not be staying in Hope Haven after this was all over.

This morning, he hadn't been in control. And that terrified him more than the explosion.

Whoever had planted that bomb hadn't just come to scare them. They'd come to kill. And if they were willing to blow up a patrol vehicle in broad daylight, then they weren't going to stop until someone was dead.

After the blast, Station Two had been the first to arrive— Grant Miller behind the wheel, his team already moving before the rig came to a full stop. Carter had arrived moments later with two deputies in tow. Ethan had given his statement, then they'd taken Sienna's. By the time the fire was extinguished, the scene processed, their statements taken, the charred wreckage hauled off the property by Weller's Towing crew and the last patrol unit cleared from the drive, it had been late afternoon. Then they'd showered off the stench of smoke, had a quick lunch, packed up the SUV and hit the road. It was seventy miles to Elk Ridge, and they were making good time.

"I've been thinking about what Jack said about my dad." Sienna's quiet voice broke the silence.

He met her gaze briefly before turning back to the road. Her hazel eyes were dull—clouded with exhaustion—and, in that moment, he would have done almost anything to see the sparkle, the laughter, back in them.

From his periphery he saw Sienna shake her head, her gaze fixed on him. "It's impossible. It doesn't make sense. Dead people don't hire semitrucks."

"I agree." He checked the mirror again, a constant habit since they'd left the ranch. The road behind them was empty. "There's no way he paid for that truck. Someone's using his name. His accounts."

She exhaled a breath that sounded like it had been held for miles. "That's what I was thinking. Someone's using his identity to cover their tracks. Maybe if we can see the records he kept, we might find something that points to who he was working with." Ethan glanced at her in time to see her finger-comb her hair back from her face—a habit she'd had when she was on edge. "I'll call Uncle Mason and ask about Dad's records. I'm thinking since he took over the ranch, he would've kept everything."

"Only one way to find out." He eased off the gas as they rounded a bend in the road. "Call him. The sooner we know what your dad was tied up in, the better."

Sienna reached for her phone, hesitating just a second before unlocking it. He glanced at her. She looked tense but determined. His lungs squeezed. They were running out of room for mistakes. His gaze flicked to the rearview mirror, checking on Nathan.

He'd almost lost them.

The thought rooted itself deep in his gut. Ethan exhaled slowly, his grip tightening on the wheel as something fierce and immovable settled in his chest. Sienna and Nathan were his family. He would do everything to protect them.

He didn't have all the answers. But he had a reason to fight—and no intention of losing them again. And for the first time in years, Ethan wasn't praying for the past to come back. He was asking for strength to move toward whatever came next.

Sienna stared at the snowcaps and the jagged sky breaking above the pines. The mountains loomed on the horizon, cold, sharp and distant. She hadn't spoken to Uncle Mason since before she'd left for Idaho. Hadn't called when she found out her dad had died, not even when the weight of loss pressed so hard it stole her breath.

She'd told herself it was because she was grieving. But really, it was guilt. Guilt over leaving Ethan. Over keeping Nathan from him. Over vanishing without a word.

Her father and Mason had been close. More than brothers—they'd been best friends. Jacob had looked up to Mason, and Mason had always been protective of his little brother. If Uncle Mason was angry at her for disappearing without a goodbye… she couldn't blame him. She just prayed he'd let her look through her dad's papers. But if he didn't take her call—or worse, shut her down—she didn't know what they'd do next.

She bit the inside of her cheek and glanced at the phone in her lap, thumb hovering over his contact.

Ethan's voice broke through her thoughts. "Don't tell him where we're going."

She looked over at him, surprised.

"We can't afford to trust anyone." His eyes were focused on the road, but she saw the tension in his jaw and in the set of his shoulders. "Not until we know who's behind this." He flicked a glance toward her. "If someone is using your dad's accounts, it could go deeper than we think."

A knot of unease coiled in her stomach. "Ethan, this is Uncle

Mason. The man who carried me on his shoulders when I was little and tickled me until I couldn't breathe. We can trust him."

Ethan rubbed his forehead. "If Mason's clean, we'll know soon enough."

She swallowed hard, a small tremor threading through her. "He's the one family member I still have left in Hope Haven."

Ethan's jaw clenched, and when he finally looked at her, his gaze hit cold and sharp. "Is he?"

A weight settled behind her ribs. "I didn't mean… I meant—"

"I know what you meant." He exhaled roughly. "Just make the call."

She knew Ethan was right. They couldn't trust anyone right now. But the idea of lying to—or even withholding information from—her uncle made her stomach turn.

Still, she tapped her screen and brought the phone to her ear, pulse thudding while it rang.

A glance at Ethan caught the wave of irritation rolling off him. She hadn't meant to hurt him. Hadn't even realized how the words might've sounded. *He's the only family I have left in Hope Haven.* But she'd seen the way Ethan flinched, the way his jaw tightened, his knuckles white around the steering wheel.

Of course Ethan was family.

He always had been. From the first moment he kissed her in the barn loft at eighteen, to the moment he proposed, to the second Nathan looked up at her with those same blue eyes.

She just hadn't thought he'd still want to be.

Not after everything she'd done.

Each ring on the other end of the line stretched tight across her nerves as she waited for the call to connect. She could still picture Uncle Mason at the ranch, arms crossed, boots dusty, voice rough-hewn like a grizzly bear. He'd always been the steady one—the one people listened to when everything else went sideways. Even her dad. Especially her dad.

When she was little, she used to think Mason knew everything. How to do complex math. How to calm a spooked horse. How to make her laugh when she skinned her knees.

Now she just hoped he remembered how to forgive.

Finally, a familiar voice answered. "Mason Blake."

His voice hit her like a jolt—craggy, unmistakably familiar. Her pulse stumbled. Her breath caught. The deep voice sent a rush of memories surging through her. The smell of hay and motor oil. His booming laugh. The way he used to ruffle her hair and call her "kid." Her throat tightened.

She shifted in her seat. "Uncle Mason…it's me. Sienna."

He paused so long she thought he'd hung up, then his voice warmed instantly. "Well, I'll be. Sienna, it's great to hear your voice. I thought I was hearing ghosts."

She blinked hard, pulse skipping. "I'm sorry I didn't call… before."

"Didn't think I'd ever hear your voice again, kid."

Her fingers curled tight around the phone. "I know. I should've called." The words came out hushed. She glanced at Ethan. He was sitting close enough to hear both sides of her conversation.

"I reckon you should've." Mason's gruff exhale echoed down the line. "You disappeared, kiddo. I wasn't sure if you'd ever come back." His voice dipped, just enough to stir fresh guilt. "Your daddy missed you."

Her dad had told her to stay low—contact no one. Had he really missed her? Pain speared her in the chest. "I—I missed him, too." Her fingers twisted in the hem of her shirt. "I'm sorry I haven't been in contact. I wanted to. I just…didn't know what to say."

Ethan glanced her way, but he didn't speak. Just drove on, his attention once again focused on the road ahead and behind them.

Mason's rough-grained voice lost some of its gravel. "Don't need to say anything. You're calling now. That's what matters."

She closed her eyes, let that small grace steady her. "I need your help. I was wondering if you kept any of Dad's old records."

Mason paused, then cleared his throat. "Sure, I did. I boxed them all up when we moved some things around last spring. Didn't have the heart to toss any of it. Why?"

She glanced at Ethan. He met her gaze with a cocked eyebrow. He didn't have to speak. She read the message in his electric blue eyes: *Don't trust anyone.* "I'm working on something. Just need to cross-reference a few things. Would it be okay to come by the ranch to look through them?"

Mason paused again. "You're in Hope Haven?"

Her pulse kicked. She could almost hear Ethan's deep voice whispering in her ear. *Don't. Trust. Anyone.* "I'm…passing through." She hated being so secretive, especially with her uncle. But Ethan had a point.

"You're welcome to stop by anytime."

Relief settled into her chest like warm sunlight. "Thanks, Uncle Mason."

"You don't have to thank me, kid. I've missed you."

She swallowed past the tightness in her throat. "I've missed you, too."

"I've got to go, but it's good to hear your voice again. You let me know when you're coming, all right? Door's always open."

"Thank you, I will." With heart still thudding, she ended the call and held the phone like it was her only connection to her favorite uncle.

Ethan glanced over.

She met his gaze. "He said yes."

Sienna stared down at her phone, Mason's number still glowing on the screen before it dimmed and disappeared. Her fingers tightened around the device before she slowly set it face down on her thigh. The SUV hummed quietly around them, tires eating up asphalt as the miles slipped by.

The call had gone better than she expected. And somehow, that only made her feel worse.

She'd expected anger. A door slammed shut. A bitter reminder of what she'd walked away from. But Mason had welcomed her like no time had passed—warm, open, forgiving. It should've lifted something off her chest. Instead, the guilt pressed in harder.

She tipped her head against the headrest and watched the blur of trees whip by. Guilt had become a familiar companion these past years. But sitting here, beside Ethan, the man she'd left without explanation, it pulsed like a bruise. She could feel his gaze flick to her and away again. Could feel the quiet weight of everything still unsaid.

Her fingers curled into her lap.

The worst part? She wasn't sure she deserved the kindness Mason had offered. And she was even less sure she deserved the second chance Ethan hadn't actually offered at all.

"I didn't mean it." She turned her head, still resting against the headrest.

Ethan didn't glance at her, but the set of his shoulders shifted slightly.

"That thing I said earlier. About Mason being the only family I had left." She drew in a breath, forcing it past the knot in her throat. "You were my family, too. You still are. I just… I didn't think you'd see it that way. Not after everything."

More silence. The trees thinned ahead, giving way to open fields and distant barns.

She looked at him then, really looked at the tired lines around his eyes, the grim set of his jaw, the way his hands flexed and stilled on the steering wheel.

"I just wanted you to know…" She closed her eyes for a moment. "In case it matters."

Time seemed suspended before Ethan finally spoke, his voice gentle, steady. "It matters."

The way he said it made the backs of her eyes sting. She hadn't expected forgiveness—not today. Maybe not ever. But she'd take that sliver of hope and hold it close.

In silence, Sienna watched the landscape shift—less forest, more sky. The early May sun glinted off stretches of barbed wire fencing, casting a golden sheen over the landscape.

Her thoughts swirled around the phone call. Mason's voice still echoed in her ears.

Nathan stirred in the back seat, murmuring in his sleep. Sienna twisted just enough to check on him. Still out. Still safe.

She looked over at Ethan. He looked as tired as she felt, which wasn't surprising considering how little sleep they'd had. She couldn't wait to get to the safety of the cabin. "How long do you think we'll need to stay at the cabin?"

Ethan glanced her way, his hand flexing slightly on the wheel. "Depends what Carter finds. If we can get a break in the case, something that gives us a direction…"

She nodded, fingers tracing the hem of her sleeve. "I'd like to go to Blake Ranch as soon as possible. If there's something in my dad's records that can help us…"

"I'll get you there." His voice was low, but she didn't miss the tightness beneath the words. He looked at her again, this time his eyes lingered for a beat longer. "I just want to be sure it's safe first."

She dropped her gaze, heart twisting with everything she wished she could take back. "Mother's Day is coming up on Sunday. I wouldn't want you to miss spending it with your mom."

The corners of his mouth lifted, just barely. "She'd understand."

"Still, I'm sorry."

"You've got nothing to be sorry for. It's not your fault someone is trying to harm you."

She looked out the window at a field of cattle grazing behind a barbed wire fence, a windmill turning lazily in the breeze.

They crested a small hill and rounded a bend. Up ahead, a rusted blue pickup sat in the center of the road. Hood up. Driver's door open. Angled just enough to make passing impossible.

Ethan eased off the gas, checked his mirrors. The road was too narrow to go around. Fenced pasture on either side left no room to maneuver.

Sienna sat up straighter, a pulse of unease tightening her muscles. "What is it?"

Ethan scanned the roadside, his eyes sharp, assessing. "Don't know. Something's off."

The SUV crept forward.

Sienna leaned closer to the windshield. "Is someone—"

Ethan reached across and pressed a hand to her shoulder. "Get down!"

Sienna's heart lurched. Before she could move, a figure rose from the far side of the pickup.

She caught the flash of metal a second before gunfire exploded.

EIGHT

Ethan yanked the gearshift into Reverse and slammed his foot to the floor. The SUV jolted backward with a screech, tires spinning on the asphalt. Bullets struck the hood, punched through the windshield with spiderweb fractures and a burst of glass.

Sienna screamed, shielding her head as she twisted, trying to protect Nathan at the same time.

"Stay down." Ethan reached across and urged her down with one hand while steering with the other. The wheel jerked under his grip. The vehicle recoiled as another round ripped through the driver's side mirror.

Nathan's cry from the back seat cut through the SUV's interior, shooting a fresh dose of adrenaline into Ethan's veins. "Down, Nathan! Keep your head down!"

"Mommy!"

Head low, Sienna awkwardly reached back a hand, trying to comfort her little boy. "It's okay, peanut, just lie down and don't move."

As Ethan scanned the woods beyond the shattered windshield, something shifted in the trees. A flash of movement caught his eye—a figure in a camo hunting jacket darting between the pines, too fast and purposeful to be a stray hiker. The rifle in his hand confirmed it. A matching figure followed close behind.

A chill crawled up Ethan's spine.

This wasn't a crime of opportunity. These men weren't fleeing. They were positioning.

Ethan's instincts kicked in, honed from years in law enforcement. Whoever was behind this knew the terrain, knew their route and had come prepared.

Ethan heard the low roar of an engine, and his gaze snapped to the rearview mirror just as a low black muscle car exploded through the fence behind them, its wide tires chewing up the field as it hurtled straight toward the road in a spray of splintered wood and dirt. The engine's deep, aggressive growl sent a shot of urgency through him.

The driver of the pickup hopped in behind the wheel and threw the pickup into motion—straight at them.

They were boxing them in. This was an ambush.

Ethan yanked the hand brake and cranked the wheel. The SUV whipped into a hard spin, tires screaming across the asphalt. The back end skidded, the entire cabin rocking with the force of the turn, jerking them sideways. His shoulder slammed against the door. The seat belt dug into his ribs.

The SUV came around fast, nose swinging back toward the way they came—the bend and the thickening forest beyond—and now faced the muscle car.

It wasn't slowing.

It bore down on them, front end low, engine howling. Whoever was behind the wheel wasn't bluffing.

Ethan gritted his teeth. A head-on hit might not total the SUV, but it could deploy the airbags, jar the engine, pin them in place—and Nathan was in the back seat. Ethan couldn't take that chance.

He had to strike first. Clip the corner just enough to knock the car off course without stopping their momentum. Risky, but better than getting trapped.

"Hold on." He slammed the gas pedal to the floor. The SUV

surged forward. The front corner clipped the muscle car's fender with a teeth-rattling jolt. Metal shrieked.

The impact rocked the SUV sideways, the vibration humming up through the steering column as they scraped past. The wheel jerked violently as he fought to keep them from sliding off the shoulder and crashing through brush at the forest's edge.

The car spun out behind them, tires screeching as it lost traction on the road and entered the path of the oncoming pickup.

Behind them, the metallic bark of more shots rang out, rounds pinging off the SUV. One took out the rear window, shattering it in a burst of glass.

Nathan cried out.

Ethan's chest cinched tight. He pushed harder on the gas and angled the vehicle toward the second cluster of trees.

Another shot slammed into Ethan's back tire. The vehicle jolted, veering sideways. He gritted his teeth, fought the wheel, and forced the SUV forward another fifty yards. He cut hard right and dove into the dense thicket. Branches slammed against the frame. Something cracked near the side mirror. The wind roared through the space where the windshield had been, flinging dust and pine needles into the cabin. The SUV bounced over uneven ground. He hit the brake just before they slammed into the trunk of a tree, then killed the engine. The smell of scorched rubber, engine heat, pine and churned-up earth filled the vehicle.

The muscle car's engine growled behind them—low, guttural and closing in fast. Judging by the speed, they'd be overtaken in minutes.

Ethan scanned the woods, mapping the terrain. The SUV was done—windshield gone, back window blown out, tire shredded. Red warning lights blinked across the dash. They couldn't stay here.

"We need to ditch the truck."

Sienna was already out of the SUV and had pulled Nathan

into her arms. He was sobbing and clinging to her neck like a lifeline. The sound of his distress hit Ethan like a punch to the chest.

"Go downhill. Stay low." He pointed east. "Head for that rock outcrop. I'll meet you there."

Sienna's brows creased. "Aren't you coming with us?"

"I'll be right behind you." He squeezed her hand, the soft warmth of her skin anchoring him for a heartbeat. "I promise." He reached into the center console, pulled out his backup Glock. "I just need thirty seconds. Go."

Sienna hesitated for a second longer, looking conflicted, her eyes brimming with tears, then she gathered Nathan more securely and headed into the trees.

Ethan reached into the back, yanked out his rifle bag, grabbed a few energy bars, then retrieved his ammo from a side panel. He crouched low, pressing his back to the vehicle, concentrating on keeping his breathing slow and controlled. Fear wanted to crawl up his spine, but he pushed it down. The muscle car's engine cut out. Seconds later, heavy footsteps rustled through the wooded area—twenty, maybe thirty yards off to his right. Voices filtered through the trees.

Someone shouted, "They can't have got far."

Another voice answered. "Check those trees!"

Carefully, Ethan moved away from the SUV and ducked behind the nearest tree trunk, weapon raised.

A figure emerged ten yards ahead at the edge of the clearing. Camo jacket, rifle in hand, scanning the woods. It was one of the men Ethan had seen running through the trees earlier. His buddies must've picked him up before giving chase.

He hadn't seen Ethan yet.

Ethan released a slow breath.

A shot gorged a chunk out of the tree he was hiding behind. Another hit just above his head. They had his location.

Ethan returned fire.

The shot echoed through the trees. The man cried out. His weapon flew out of his hand, and he clutched his shoulder, staggering backward before hitting the ground. More shouts erupted. But Ethan was already moving—circling wide, keeping low, putting distance between himself and the SUV. If he could draw the others away, it would give Sienna time to disappear into the forest.

Sienna crouched behind the rock outcrop, pressing her back against the cold rough stone as she kept Nathan down low beside her—one arm wrapped tightly around his trembling body, the other braced against the dry pine needles that littered the ground. The rock jutted out from the hillside like a natural wall. Its solid presence was a comfort and a threat all at once. The outcrop gave them cover. But it wouldn't hold up to bullets if they were spotted. If anyone passed along the slope above, she needed to stay invisible.

She heaved in a deep breath, then released it slowly, trying to calm her insides. She'd been running on instinct and adrenaline, and she couldn't stop shaking. Her heart pounded so hard it was making the front of her shirt vibrate.

Nathan peeked up at her, his eyes red-rimmed, his small face streaked with dirt. She smoothed away his tears with her thumbs. "Don't be scared, peanut, we're going to be okay."

"Are the bad men coming, Mommy?" he whispered, as if understanding the importance of being as quiet as they could.

"No, baby, they won't find us." That had been her constant prayer since she left Ethan half an hour ago.

Careful not to shift too high above the ridge line, she peeked over the top of the rock.

Where was Ethan? He'd said he needed thirty seconds. He should've been right behind them.

Unless…she refused to let the thought—and the fear that followed close behind—consume her. She'd heard gunshots, but it didn't mean that Ethan had been…that he was…

She pushed the thought away. She couldn't afford to think like that. God had them. He wouldn't let anything happen to Ethan.

Lord, please let him be okay. Cover him in Your protection and bring him safely back to us.

Moments later, Ethan appeared, Glock in hand, rifle bag slung over one shoulder. Relief coursed through her at the sight of him alive and unharmed.

He dropped to a knee beside them, next to the spindly fir tree that leaned crookedly beside the outcrop. Its roots tangled around the base like it had grown there on instinct.

His gaze ran over her and Nathan. "Are the two of you okay?" He stroked his hand over Nathan's head.

She nodded, not trusting herself to speak in case she broke down again. She was still deeply embarrassed by the way she'd cried all over him this morning.

As if sensing how fragile she was feeling, he gently brushed his hand against her arm. "Come on, we need to keep moving."

"Are they still following?" Even to her own ears, her voice sounded thready.

"I lost them." Ethan scanned the ridge. "But that doesn't mean they've stopped looking. We need to get off this trail before they figure out where we are." He glanced at Sienna, then beyond her to the treetops. "There's a cabin about two miles back. I saw it when we passed through the thinning trees before the ambush."

She gathered Nathan, preparing to move on Ethan's command. "Maybe it's occupied and we can get help."

"Maybe. Or it could be a ranger's cabin. Either way, it's shelter. We'll regroup there, try to get a signal. Maybe they'll have a vehicle we can borrow."

She cradled Nathan close, using her hands and body to shield him. "How much farther to Elk Ridge? Couldn't we just go there?"

Ethan checked his smartwatch. "Forty miles. Too far to cover. Especially on foot." His gaze met hers. "Wouldn't surprise me if those guys already have the cabin on their radar. How else would they have known to set up an ambush on this stretch of road?"

Sienna's brow furrowed. "But how did they even find out where we were headed?"

"That's an excellent question. One I've been asking myself." He paused, scanning the woods again. "There's only one answer—we have a mole."

Her stomach dropped. "How? Who?"

"I don't know." His tone was clipped, controlled. He did another sweep of their surroundings. "Come on. Stay low. Let's head for the trees on that side." He pointed west, then brushed his hands over the fallen pine needles and dried leaves, trying to obscure their trail.

Somewhere behind them, a squirrel scurried through the underbrush—the sound jarring in the silence. Sienna startled so violently she nearly lost her grip on Nathan.

"It's okay." Ethan gave her a quick grounding hug. "We'll be okay." He secured his Glock in the back waistband of his cargo pants. "I'll carry him."

Sienna hesitated. Her maternal instinct wanted her to keep Nathan in her arms, where she could protect him. But deep down, she knew Ethan had a better shot at keeping him safe.

She handed him over.

The forest closed around them, thick with pine and shadow. The sunlight filtering through the canopy came in faint, broken shafts, and the hush was almost too deep as they trekked over brittle leaves and dirt packed hard by wind and weather.

Ethan adjusted Nathan's weight against his chest and kept his steps light on the soft carpet of needles. Sienna moved beside him, careful but fast, her hand brushing Nathan's back every now and then as if to reassure him she was still there.

Nathan's breathing was slowing, but his grip around Ethan's neck hadn't relaxed.

They'd gone maybe a quarter mile when Ethan heard a noise that had him raising a hand, halting them with a silent signal. Sienna stopped mid-step.

He crouched, shifting Nathan into his arms more securely.

Footsteps. Someone was moving through the trees behind them. Slow. Deliberate.

Ethan turned toward Sienna and mouthed, *Down.*

She followed him as he dropped behind a fallen moss-covered log.

The footsteps drew closer.

He met Sienna's gaze. She covered her mouth, looking like her nerves were stretched so taut she might give into panic at any second. Hardly daring to breathe, he reached out and gently brushed back a lock of hair that had escaped her ponytail, hoping to lend her strength with his touch.

One of the men called out, his voice low but cutting. "Spread out."

Another voice farther away answered. "You sure they didn't head east?"

"No. I saw boot prints going downhill."

Sienna's eyes widened. Ethan pressed a finger to his lips and kept Nathan tucked close against his chest, shielding him from view.

A twig snapped just beyond the log.

Sienna flinched. Nathan reached out to her, but, thankfully, didn't make a sound. She took him, freeing Ethan's hands.

Ethan reached slowly for his Glock, though every movement felt magnified in the stillness. His heartbeat pulsed hard in his ears. The man was so close Ethan could hear him breathing, smell his cologne—sharp and out of place in the pine-scented forest air.

Nathan gave a tiny whimper. Sienna rocked him gently.

If God had heard Ethan's prayer this morning before his patrol truck exploded, maybe He might hear Ethan again. He closed his eyes and sent up a silent prayer. *Please, Lord, if You can hear me, quiet Nathan's spirit. Cover us now. Don't let these men find us.*

The footsteps paused.

Ethan lay on his back, his heart hammering. But he was ready if a face appeared above them. He wasn't going to let anyone take Nathan—or Sienna—from him.

Seconds that felt like hours ticked by, then, finally, the man turned away. Another branch snapped as he moved off, muttering into a walkie-talkie. "Nothing. Checking the lower slope."

Only after the voices faded completely did Ethan breathe again. He sat up, met Sienna's eyes. Her lashes were damp, but her mouth was set in a firm line.

He whispered, "You okay?"

She nodded. "Let's keep going."

They rose carefully and pressed deeper into the forest, taking a wider angle now—less direct but safer. Ethan scanned the trees constantly, every rustle setting his nerves on edge.

They wouldn't be safe until they were behind a locked door.

He glanced down at Nathan. "Give him to me."

This time Sienna didn't hesitate before letting Ethan take him. Nathan curled into his arms without hesitation. "Let's move. We'll rest once we're inside the cabin."

Sienna fell in step beside him. They moved through the thickening trees. Ethan adjusted his grip on his son and kept a constant awareness of his surroundings. He was going to find out who was behind this. And if, indeed, there was a mole, he'd discover who it was, too. But, right now, his only job was to keep his family safe.

NINE

Ethan knocked on the cabin's door for the second time.

Still no answer.

Sienna shifted her stance, trying to ease the strain in her back. Nathan had gone quiet in her arms after Ethan handed him over just before they stepped onto the porch, but his grip hadn't loosened. He clung to her, his face buried against her neck, his little body heavy with exhaustion.

"Do you think it's unoccupied?"

"Looks that way." Ethan strode around the side of the veranda.

Sienna followed and occasionally glanced behind them. They'd been walking for nearly an hour, and she was completely turned around—unable to pinpoint where they were.

Ethan didn't seem to have that problem. "I don't see anyone inside."

She turned to find him peering through the window.

This wasn't the cabin Ethan had spotted from the road and told her about. This one sat deeper in the woods, hidden behind a ridge, tucked so far back they'd nearly walked past it. They'd been on their way to the other cabin when Ethan had noticed a flicker of roofline through a break in the trees, and they'd come to see if someone could help. But so far, the place seemed empty.

"Looks like a vacation rental." He pulled a slim multitool

from the side pocket of his cargo pants. "Doesn't look lived in." He returned to the front and crouched before the weathered cabin door. He worked the lock with quick, focused movements. Within seconds, there was a soft *click*.

He stood, eased the door open and waited a beat.

When no occupants appeared, he glanced back at Sienna. "Wait here while I check it out."

Sienna's heart dove into her boots. She didn't want to remain out there alone. By all accounts, the cabin was empty, but somewhere behind them, men were searching with murder in mind.

She took a hurried step forward. "I'm coming with you."

"Stay behind me." Ethan entered the cabin on full alert.

Sienna quietly shut the door behind them, then followed Ethan. If the cabin was empty, she didn't want to risk anyone walking in behind them unnoticed.

The cabin smelled faintly of woodsmoke, old pine and lemon oil. Dust floated in the slanted light as Sienna stepped farther into the narrow living room behind Ethan, her gaze drifting over the cozy couch, the stone fireplace and a bookshelf half-filled with paperbacks and board games. The furniture was clean, coordinated—not luxurious but warm and well maintained.

To the right, the kitchen opened up—small, neat and, by the looks of it, stocked. Someone had left a welcome basket of tea, cocoa and cookies by the stove, making her agree with Ethan that it was a vacation rental currently between guests.

Sienna stayed close behind him, Nathan heavy in her arms, his breath warm against her neck. Her own pulse still hadn't settled. But the deeper they moved into the cabin, the more the panic began to ease its grip.

"Clear so far." Ethan kept his voice low, nodded toward the short hallway. "Bedroom and bathroom."

The first door he opened turned out to be the bedroom. It was simple but inviting. A queen bed topped with a quilt in soft shades of cream and mint green sat beneath the window.

A nightstand held a lamp with a stained-glass shade. Sunlight cut across the floorboards in a warm stripe. This was a place meant for slow mornings and coffee in bed. He checked the closet, under the bed, then crossed the room and checked the window locks as he scanned outside.

"Clear."

She followed him to the second door but stayed in the hall, peeking inside. Though small, the space was charming. Warm cream tiles lined the walls, and a khaki green bath mat lay in front of a bathtub/shower combo with a shower curtain patterned in pinecones and forest greenery. A shelf on the opposite wall held neatly rolled towels, and above the toilet, a few rolls of toilet paper sat neatly on the shelf above the tank.

Ethan pushed back the curtain, checked the lock on the window. "Clear."

The final knot in Sienna's chest loosened with the breath she expelled. The cabin seemed safe enough—if she didn't think too hard about how easily Ethan had gained access.

"I need to put him down." Nathan had fallen asleep and was too heavy for her to continue to carry.

After settling him in the middle of the bed, she found Ethan in the kitchen standing in front of the open pantry door.

He glanced over his shoulder. "It's not overflowing, but it's stocked with enough to get by for a few days."

Noticing that he'd stowed the rifle bag and ammo on a high shelf where Nathan couldn't reach them, she went over and looked past him into the pantry. Canned goods lined the shelves—soups, beans, chili, dry goods, a jar of peanut butter, boxes of crackers and bottled water.

In these areas, cabin owners usually left their pantries stocked in case someone got stranded in bad weather. Sienna sent up a silent *Thank You* to God for the kind-hearted, compassionate people who took the trouble to care for others.

On the fridge door was a small magnet with the Wi-Fi details.

"Look." She plucked it from the fridge. "The Wi-Fi password."

"That's great." He pulled out his phone, waiting for Sienna to share the password. "What is it?"

She stared at the red X beside the Wi-Fi information. "I don't think it's working." She turned the magnet for him to see. "It's crossed out."

"That means the Wi-Fi's down." He held up his phone, strolling toward the door. "Out here, it was probably spotty to begin with."

He moved to the window and paused beside the sage-green gingham curtains. "I've got nothing. You?"

Sienna placed the magnet back on the fridge, withdrew her phone from the back pocket of her jeans and inspected it.

"No." She met his gaze, realization sinking like a heavy stone in her stomach. "We can't call for help."

"Then we don't count on help coming. We stay vigilant."

Trying not to let fresh panic overtake her, Sienna sank onto a chair at the small kitchen table. "Do you think they'll find us?"

Ethan ran a hand through his hair and slipped his phone into his breast pocket. "If we hadn't stumbled on this cabin, we would never have known it was here. Chances are, they'll head for the other cabin. It's the only one noticeable from the road, and they'd think we went there."

A shudder ran through her. They *had* been heading there. Thank God they happened upon this one instead.

"So, you don't think they'll find us?" She knew Ethan didn't know any more than she did, but she needed his reassurance.

As if he sensed that, he sauntered over to the table and pulled out a chair opposite hers. "If they do, we'll be ready."

Just that small guarantee, spoken with such commanding authority, gave her peace. She nodded, hugging her arms around herself. "Okay."

Hours later, with no sign of the men following them, Ethan began to breathe a little easier. He'd secured the cabin, walked the perimeter and found no evidence anyone else had been in the vicinity.

Nathan had woken from his nap hungry but surprisingly calm once he'd found Ethan with Sienna in the kitchen. They had soup and crackers for dinner, while Ethan enjoyed listening as his son brought him up to speed on the latest episode of his favorite cartoon, leaving him with a gut-deep longing to know everything about this little boy who looked so much like him.

As much as he would've loved to listen to Nathan talk all night, the little boy had been so wrung out from the day that he had nodded off shortly after finishing his hot chocolate.

Now, alone with Sienna at the sink, Ethan found himself trying to come up with a way to ease into the topic most prominent in his mind. He glanced at her as he rinsed a bowl, then handed it off. The fire crackled softly behind them, casting flickers of gold across the kitchen walls. He reached for another bowl while Sienna dried the one he'd handed her with a dish towel, then set it on the counter.

Shoulders tight, he rinsed the last bowl, placed it in the drainer, then leaned on the edge of the sink and wiped his hands slowly on a dish towel. Beside him, Sienna dried the bowl, her movements unhurried, thoughtful, then she added it to the small stack on the counter.

He glanced toward the bedroom door where Nathan was sound asleep. "What was it like?"

Sienna stilled, her brows drawing together above her attractive hazel eyes. "What was what like?"

He folded the dish towel, dropped it onto the counter, then

crossed his arms over his chest. "The pregnancy. Finding out. Giving birth. All of it."

She stared at him with such sudden stillness, he knew his question had caught her completely off guard. The silence stretched for thirty long, slow seconds before she set her towel beside his and leaned back against the counter.

"I didn't even know at first." She let out a slow breath. "I didn't find out until I was nearly four months along."

Her words knocked the wind out of his chest. "Four months?"

She gave a faint nod. "I thought the stress had thrown my cycle out of whack. I felt tired, off, sick every now and then, but I told myself it was the emotional fallout from everything I'd just left behind. I wasn't showing. And I didn't want to believe it. Not until I could no longer ignore the signs."

"I'm sorry." Deep down, he knew he was to blame. They'd been engaged. He'd been completely in love with her and felt already married to her in every way that counted. For sure, he knew he'd never want to grow old with any other woman. And Sienna had told him she felt the same. Back then, neither of them had been walking with the Lord. He'd proposed when she was twenty-one and he twenty-four. She'd been in her final year of undergrad and had wanted to wait until she graduated. If he'd had his way, he would've married her the day he proposed. They'd been young and foolish. Only two months away from their wedding day, they should've waited. But if they had, she would've left, and he wouldn't have Nathan.

A strange ache moved through his chest. When she left, he didn't just lose her. He lost the future he thought they had. "Were you scared?"

Sienna gave a soft chuckle. "Terrified."

She might make light of it, but the word still landed like a punch. She'd faced it without him.

"Did you have anyone? Or were you completely alone?" The thought of her being on her own twisted in his gut.

She gave a one-shoulder shrug. "At first. Then I made friends. But that didn't make it easy." Her gaze met his, and the look in her eyes made his heart turn over. "Especially when I started thinking about how I'd raise him. About what I'd say when he started asking questions."

Ethan's throat burned. "Did he ever ask about me?"

She smiled, even if it was a little sad around the edges. "He does. A lot." Her voice softened. "I told him his daddy helps people. That he's a brave cop. And that he loves him very much—even if he can't be with us."

His breath left him in a quiet rush. "Thank you."

"I knew that if you had any idea he existed, you'd love him as much as I do."

He looked down at his boots, then back toward the closed bedroom door. "He's amazing."

She smiled softly. "He's my everything." She tucked a stray lock of hair behind her ear. "He's already very attached to you, Ethan."

"And I to him." He cleared the sudden thickness in his throat. "I want to know all about him. His first word. When he took his first step. What makes him laugh. His favorite everything. I want it all, Sienna. I want to know my son."

She glanced down, then back at him, her eyes overbright as she reached for her bottled water. "Then let's start with the day he was born."

Ethan nodded, throat tight.

He didn't know how to reclaim the years he'd missed, but he was going to try.

Sienna shifted slightly on the couch beside Ethan, their shoulders not quite touching. The fire crackled softly, filling the cabin with a hush, as if the world had narrowed to this moment. A stillness that she hadn't known in years settled in her chest.

Over water and then coffee, she'd told him everything she

could think of about their son, had answered all his questions. He had laughed at the funny parts, had squeezed her hand gently, lending her compassion at the hard parts. He'd listened without flinching, asked without accusation. There was no bitterness in him, just that steady strength he'd always carried like it was stitched into his bones. Not for show. Not for pride. Just part of who he was.

Finally, he sat back, his gaze sincere. "You've done a wonderful job with raising him."

"Thank you."

How had she ever walked away from this man?

She used to tell herself that leaving had been the only way to keep him safe. But sitting here now, with him so close and still somehow out of reach, all she could feel was the ache of what she'd lost. A future she could never get back. The day he asked her to marry him had been the happiest day of her life. She wished she hadn't insisted they wait until she finished her studies in equine science. Wished they'd just gone ahead and gotten married and worked out the rest afterward. But she'd worried that if she hadn't waited, she might have given up her dreams to become a wife and mother instead, the way her mom had. Never to recognize her full potential. And so she had asked Ethan to wait until she'd graduated. He'd been happy to accommodate her. And in the end, they had both missed out on what could've been.

Maybe that was what hurt the most—he would've stood by her, no matter what. He always had.

Because that was who Ethan was.

He came from a long line of lawmen—men who'd stood for something. His father. His grandfather and great-grandfather. And long before that, Elijah Wade Callahan—his famous great-great-great-grandfather. A frontier sheriff known for justice and mercy in equal measure. He'd held the line in Dead River, Wyoming. Faced down four outlaws without flinching and had his name in history books. The family still had his old badge, a dent in the middle where a bullet had nearly taken him out.

That was Ethan's legacy. Not loud or showy. Just solid and good.

And she'd been the fool who walked away from him.

He'd asked her if she'd be staying in Hope Haven after this was all over, and she'd said she didn't know. She loved him, but she also knew he would never truly forgive her. Not for leaving the way she had. And not for keeping his son from him.

So how could they ever have a future?

Without Ethan, there was nothing for her in Hope Haven.

She looked toward the bedroom, her chest aching. Nathan was the only thing she'd done right. And somehow, despite it all, Ethan was already finding ways to love him.

Ethan placed his empty coffee mug on the coffee table. "Has he started kindergarten?"

Sienna smiled, thinking of Nathan at kindergarten. "Yes, and he loves it. Last month, he performed a citizen's arrest on a kid in his class for jumping the line at the monkey bars. Told his teacher it was his civic duty."

Ethan let out a low chuckle, the sound rumbling deep in his chest. "You're kidding."

"I wish I were. He even made the poor kid sit out recess while he wrote an incident report in crayon."

Ethan laughed again, shaking his head. "Sounds like he's got the Callahan blood, all right."

"This morning, he asked if he could wear his Woody boots because he wants to be a sheriff today."

Ethan's grin was that of a proud father. "Looks like he'll be joining the long line of Callahan lawmen one day."

As her gaze drifted over his face, his smile softened. The firelight danced in his eyes, catching on silver flecks that hadn't been there before—or maybe she'd just forgotten how easily he could undo her with one look. Her heart gave a little flip.

As the laughter faded, something shifted between them. He wasn't smiling anymore. He was watching her—really watching her—and it was all she could do not to look away. His hand came up slowly, fingers brushing a loose strand of hair. The warmth of his touch, the gentleness of it, made her catch her breath.

He leaned in, slow and unhurried.

Sienna held her breath.

But instead of kissing her, his gaze dropped. His fingers found the hollow of her throat, and then—so carefully—it was as if he already knew what he'd find, he slipped the chain from beneath her collar.

Her breath hitched.

She followed his gaze to the delicate gold necklace now resting in his palm.

Her engagement ring.

The princess-cut sapphire glinted softly in the firelight like it still held a spark of everything they'd almost had.

His voice was low, a little rough. "You kept it."

Heart pounding like he'd just caught her committing a crime, Sienna curled her fingers around the ring and slipped it back beneath her neckline.

"Yes."

Some memories were too painful to forget, too precious to erase. Holding on to the past had a cost, and she was already paying it.

TEN

She still wore it.

Not on her hand where a woman wore a ring that said, *I belong to someone.* But hidden, strung on a gold chain and tucked away like a secret. It should've been long gone by now. Pawned. Boxed. Buried. Or even tossed in a river somewhere.

But it wasn't. It sat right over her heart.

She'd offered no explanation when he saw it. Just dropped it back beneath her shirt, muttered something about being tired and disappeared into the bedroom. He hadn't followed. Couldn't decide if he'd been too stunned or if he didn't want to find out it meant nothing. That maybe she'd put it there and forgot about it.

But if it didn't mean anything, why keep it on a chain and wear it around her neck?

Last night he'd stayed out by the fire, letting too many questions roll around in his head while he kept watch for potential danger. That ring had sat in a velvet box in his dresser for two weeks before he'd built up the nerve to give it to her. It still made him smile—made his heart thud—when he thought of how she'd wrapped her arms around his neck and shouted, *Yes!* before he even finished the question. He'd placed it on her finger with a promise of forever.

Boots crunching over the damp underbrush, he climbed the ridge. The early morning air was cool and sharp with the scent of pine and wet bark. Sunlight filtered through the canopy, catching on the dew that clung to the bramble leaves.

A new realization struck him, stopping him in mid-step. She hadn't returned the ring, and he hadn't formally ended their engagement—only called off the wedding. He raised his eyes toward the pale morning sky. Technically, Sienna was still his fiancée. He glanced back toward the cabin, where she was probably still asleep. Her keeping the ring was a mere technicality, not anything that spoke to the real state of their relationship.

He should officially break it off. She'd said herself she wasn't planning to stay. By all accounts, she was here for his help, then she'd move on. *Remember that!* He scrubbed his hands over his face, tired and cranky from too little sleep. No doubt they'd work out a mutually agreeable arrangement so he could stay in Nathan's life. He might not be able to forgive her, but his son mattered more than any grievance, and Ethan would do whatever it took to help raise Nathan from here on out.

Reaching the tree line, Ethan paused, letting his gaze sweep the terrain. Nothing moved. No fresh tracks, no broken branches. He'd already walked the perimeter once before sunrise and nothing had changed. Whoever had opened fire on them yesterday hadn't circled back in the night. A fair guess said they'd pulled out—at least for now.

Stepping into a clearing, he reached for his phone and tilted it above his head. One bar flickered in the top corner, and he breathed a sigh of relief. He needed to call Carter and Weller's Towing. The phone buzzed in his hand before he could make the call.

He thumbed the green answer icon on the second ring. "Carter, I was just about to call you."

Carter's breath whooshed out. "I've been trying to reach you since yesterday. I expected you to check in. When you didn't, I tried calling, but your phone kept going to voicemail."

"We ran into a bit of trouble on the way up here. I haven't

had a signal until now." Ethan leaned a shoulder against a pine and raked a hand through his hair.

"Are you at the cabin?" Carter's voice crackled on the line.

Ethan shifted for a better signal. "We're at *a* cabin, just not the one in Elk Ridge."

"What happened?"

"Yesterday, about three miles west of Hollow Ridge Road, on the way to Elk Ridge, we drove into an ambush."

Carter drew in a sharp breath, then gave a low whistle. "Tell me you guys are okay."

"We're fine, but the SUV is out of commission. We had to abandon it."

"Where are you now?"

"We headed west and found a vacation cabin tucked off the trail. Looks like it's between renters."

"How did anyone know you'd be on that stretch of road at that time?"

Ethan pushed off the tree, started pacing. "That's the same question I have. Did you tell anyone we were heading to Elk Ridge?"

"No, Ethan! No." The outrage in Carter's voice almost convinced him.

He hadn't disclosed their plans to anyone but Carter and Sienna. Sienna didn't tell anyone else, and he hadn't, either. So that left only Jack Carter.

"I didn't tell anyone, Ethan." Carter heaved a breath. "We spoke on the phone at stupid o'clock in the morning. I didn't tell anyone."

Ethan turned a slow circle, scanning the trees. "Then explain how they found us."

"You think I gave them your location?"

"I think you're the only one who knew."

"No." Carter's voice was tight. Defensive. "I didn't tell a

soul. Not my wife. Not anyone on duty. I didn't write it down. Nothing was recorded."

"Where were you when you called to tell me the cabin was ready?"

"Here, at my desk, but no one was around."

"Are you sure?"

"Fairly sure." The sound of a chair creaking filtered through the phone. "I kept my voice low. Jennifer was working Records. She wasn't even close enough to overhear me."

Ethan watched a squirrel scurry along a branch and disappear around the tree. "Someone leaked the information. If it wasn't me, Sienna or you, who was it?"

"I don't know."

Ethan blew out a breath, frustration crawling under his skin. "Check the floor cams. Look for anyone who passed through, anyone who lingered close enough to overhear."

"I'll pull the security feeds." A rustle of papers followed his words. "You really think I shared that information?"

Ethan pinched the bridge of his nose. "I think someone knew exactly where we were headed and when. That narrows the field."

"I've been your second for four years."

Deep down, Ethan didn't want to believe that Carter would ever betray him, but nothing was adding up. If Carter was innocent, it would come to light soon enough. Ethan exhaled, hating that he doubted his friend. "I'm not accusing you, Carter. I'm asking you to help me eliminate you from the equation."

A heavy silence stretched for several seconds, then Carter let out a breath, resigned. "Fair enough." He could almost hear Carter's shrug through the phone. "The reason I was calling was to tell you that a hiker reported a burnt-out semi in that old quarry over at Hollow Ridge."

The hairs on the back of Ethan's neck prickled. "You think it's the same semi?"

"No way to tell. It's been torched completely. But how many self-driving semitrucks are around here? And the timing's close enough. The quarry is remote. Nobody goes out there unless they're hunting, hiking or lost."

Ethan squinted into the distance. "It's a little suspicious that an autonomous semi goes rogue, then a couple days later another one turns up torched to the frame. I'd guess we're looking at the same semi."

"That's not all. You remember that prescribed burn project they did out in Flathead County last month?"

"Yeah." He braced a hand against a tree trunk.

"Grant Miller was one of the firefighters who volunteered to help mark off the safe zones. Said the quarry was low risk— clean, open, nothing to catch. Just gravel and rock. Told the county it'd be perfect for controlled burns."

Ethan's brows drew down. "Ideal, if you wanted to burn something big without setting half the state alight."

"Exactly. I'm not saying he had anything to do with this. Just that it lines up too close to ignore."

Ethan glanced up as a woodpecker began tapping a steady rhythm against the bark of a nearby tree. "I want photos, soil samples, accelerant testing. Sweep for tire tracks, shoe prints— anything out of place."

"You got it."

Ethan rubbed the tension at the back of his neck. "I'll check back with you in a few hours."

"Are you staying at the rental?"

"Probably best not to. We don't know if this area is safe. And renters can turn up at any time." Right now, his ranch was the only place he could count on—the one location he could fortify.

"Send me your GPS and I'll come get you."

"Thanks. Sending it now." He scratched his chin, pulling a face at the rasp of stubble and the itch of new growth.

"Great. I'm on my way." A chair scraped on the floor and keys jingled, signaling Carter's movement.

"I'll send you the directions to the cabin, but we'll need to go get the things from my SUV."

"All right."

Ethan ended the call and thumbed through his contacts until he reached Weller's Towing to arrange retrieval of the SUV. They were literally not out of the woods yet. He'd get them through whatever came next. No matter what it took.

Sienna was dreading having to face Ethan. Ever since last night, the ring on her necklace felt as heavy as a boulder. She'd worn it for years, tucked against her heart, hidden beneath layers of cotton and guilt. Most days, she forgot it was there. But not today. Not after the way Ethan had looked at her when he saw it—like the ground had shifted beneath his feet.

Sitting with Nathan at the farmhouse table, she wrapped her hands around her coffee mug, letting the warmth seep into her palms as she watched Nathan drink his hot chocolate.

She hadn't meant for Ethan to see the ring. Hadn't been ready for the way his eyes had softened as he stared at it dangling from the end of the necklace. Or for the way her heart had stuttered in panic. She'd read the questions in his eyes and knew she wouldn't have been able to answer them. How would she explain? What would she say? That it was just a memory? That she'd placed it there for safekeeping and had forgotten about it? When in truth, it was proof that Ethan once loved her deeply. A reminder that she used to be part of a couple. Proof that she was a woman who loved and was loved.

But not anymore. Still, she couldn't bring herself to take off the necklace, give him back the ring. It was hard to let go. It would be like losing a limb or one of her senses.

"You forgot to give me the ice cream you promised." Nathan's words pulled her out of her thoughts, drawing her attention to his cheeky grin. He was swinging his legs and slurping his chocolate like he didn't have a care.

Her heart warmed. *Thank You, Father, that Nathan doesn't seem to be affected by his experiences from the last few days. Thank You that he's his usual energetic, playful self. Please don't let him have any long-term psychological problems because of this.*

She plucked a tissue from the table and smoothed away Nathan's chocolate mustache. "I didn't forget, peanut. You fell asleep. But I promise, the minute we're back home, you'll have your ice cream." Her voice was gentle, but her heart ached. Home felt a hundred miles away, and she didn't know when they'd reach it.

"Even if it's the middle of the night?"

She raised her brows. "Will you be awake?"

With a wide grin, he nodded vigorously. "Uh-huh."

Sienna chuckled and, even at five years old, Nathan must've sensed her doubt. "Can I have it for breakfast instead?"

She laughed. "We'll see."

He gave a long-suffering sigh. "That means no."

The door opened and Ethan filled the doorway, boots dusted with pine needles. He stomped his feet before stepping inside the cabin, looking like a man with the weight of the world on his shoulders. He met her gaze and sent her pulse into overdrive.

"Perimeter's clear." His attention shifted to Nathan. "What means no?"

Sienna pushed up from her chair. "He's trying to negotiate ice cream for breakfast." She reached for a fresh mug. "Coffee?"

"Thanks." He crossed the room and ruffled Nathan's hair. "Maybe we should put it to a vote." He grinned down at Nathan, his smile every bit as cheeky as their son's. "Everyone in favor of ice cream for breakfast, say aye."

It didn't surprise her when they both yelled, "Aye!" in unison.

"Everyone against, say nay."

Because the mood was lighthearted, Sienna played along. "Nay!"

Ethan ruffled Nathan's hair again. "Looks like the ayes have it, son."

Nathan giggled, but Sienna's heart paused for a count of three. How often had she dreamed of moments like this? Fun family times with Ethan when he'd laugh and call Nathan "son"? Sudden tears misted her vision, and she turned away before Ethan noticed.

She filled the mug with black coffee from the pot. "Why am I not surprised the two of you would gang up on me?" She kept her tone amused while blinking rapidly to clear her eyes.

"Can I go play?" Nathan was already scooting off the chair.

"Yes." Sienna glanced over her shoulder. "But stay inside."

"Okay." He hopped off his chair and zoomed to the bedroom. Probably to retrieve Woody.

She handed Ethan the mug of coffee. "I saw the note you left for the owners."

"Thanks." Accepting the coffee, he glanced at the fridge where the note was pinned beneath a magnet and set the mug on the table. "It's only right that we let them know we were here and leave payment."

That was what she loved about him. His sense of propriety. "I'm sure they'll appreciate it."

He nodded as he drew out a chair and sat at the table.

She removed Nathan's cup and took it to the sink to wash up. "Not sure how long the hot chocolate will keep him going. There isn't much in the way of breakfast."

"I have a few child-friendly energy bars if he gets hungry." Ethan took a measured sip. "I managed to get a signal. Carter is coming to pick us up. I also called Weller's guys to retrieve the SUV."

She'd heard when he left the cabin earlier, and she had gotten up to get ready. "How soon before they arrive?"

"We should probably leave shortly to meet Carter on the road. He has our coordinates."

After drying the cup, she stowed it in the cupboard with the others. "We're ready when you are."

He took another sip of his coffee. "A hiker found a burned-out semi at the old quarry east of here."

She closed the cupboard door slowly. "Do you think it's the one that ran us off the road?"

"I'm guessing it is. The detectives said there was no driver's seat or steering wheel. Even burnt out, they could tell it was all computerized inside. There aren't a lot of self-driving trucks on the road. The chance of this being a different vehicle is slim."

"Do you know who burned the semi?"

"Not yet. Forensics is looking at it now." He set his mug down with care. "Grant Miller flagged that quarry last month. Helped mark it for the county burn project."

She moved back to the table and took her seat, wrapping her hands around her mug. "What does that mean?"

He held her gaze. "That he knew the perfect spot to torch a rig."

Her breath caught. She'd prayed for answers, but was she ready for them?

ELEVEN

Sienna leaned against the front window of Ethan's ranch, her necklace clutched in her hand, as she watched him adjust the last camera over the porch. She tightened her grip on the ring that had once symbolized so much promise.

It was now a constant reminder of devastating loss.

Yesterday had passed in a blur of movement—trekking to the road to meet Carter and Weller's Towing, transferring their belongings from the SUV to Carter's truck, then driving back to Ethan's ranch. From the moment they returned, the activity hadn't let up. Ethan sprang into action, calling in favors and bringing in trusted men. Within hours, the ranch was transforming. He worked alongside the crew, reinforcing doors, securing windows and replacing locks. Sienna had watched them install extra floodlights, mount cameras and wire alarms around the property.

The place looked like a set from a standoff movie. Ethan was preparing for war.

Because of her.

She hadn't wanted to leave him. She'd left to keep him alive. But returning had put a target on his back.

Ethan could build all the walls he wanted around this place, but she was the breach—the reason danger kept seeping in. And yet…she wanted to stay. More than anything. Not because she was tired of running, but because she still loved the man out there on that porch.

She didn't know how to stay—not when she wasn't sure he even wanted her here. He'd made it clear he would fight for a place in Nathan's life. He hadn't said a word about needing her. And claiming their son didn't mean he forgave her.

How would she ever make up for the depth of hurt she'd caused him? She'd tried atoning for her past through good works and self-sacrifice. If she could just prove herself worthy enough, maybe God would forgive her. Maybe Ethan would, too—eventually.

"Mommy, can I go get my other toys?" Nathan's voice was light and hopeful, edged with eager innocence, pulling her back to the room.

She dropped the necklace into the neckline of her baby-blue vest top, then turned from the window. "Of course."

Nathan dashed off, leaving Sienna alone with Ethan's mom for the first time since Grace and James—Ethan's mom and dad—had arrived unexpectedly half an hour ago. Nathan bolted down the hallway, and guilt pinched at her. She'd let him pack only a few special toys when they fled—just enough to stuff in his little backpack before leaving everything they owned behind.

"He's beautiful, Sienna." Grace smiled, clasping her hands in her lap. She hadn't changed much. In fact, Sienna was sure she hadn't aged at all in six years. "He's an exact copy of Ethan at that age."

Ethan had been outside with the workmen when his parents arrived. Sienna had found herself facing Grace, bracing for the reaction she deserved after running out on Ethan only weeks before they were supposed to walk down the aisle. What she received was...well...*grace*. That was the only way to describe Grace Callahan's reaction to seeing Sienna again and meeting Nathan for the first time. She'd clearly been shocked, but then she gazed at Nathan with misty eyes as she stroked his cheek.

"Hello, sweet boy. It's lovely to meet you."

Nathan had grinned up at her, sticking out his hand in a very grown-up attempt at a handshake. "Nice to meet you, ma'am." Which had drawn a soft laugh from his grandmother.

"Does he know?" Grace didn't have to come right out now and voice the words. Sienna knew what she was asking.

Does Nathan know that Ethan is his father?

Sienna wrapped the cardigan of her matching twin set around herself. "Not yet. There hasn't been a good time so far."

Grace met her gaze with steady eyes. "Is there ever a good time?"

Sienna looked away. Deep down, she was terrified Nathan would never forgive her for hiding the truth that Ethan was his dad. And the longer she took to tell him, the harder it was becoming.

"I guess not." She wasn't looking forward to seeing the accusation in her son's blue eyes. Not yet.

Grace glanced at her watch. "It's almost time to think about dinner. Can I help you?"

Sienna blinked, caught off guard by the kindness threaded through the other woman's tone. She didn't deserve such compassion. Not after disappearing without a word, changing her number and cutting off everyone who cared. Before all that, Grace had been a second mother. Sienna had dreamed of officially becoming part of the Callahan family.

She nodded. "Thank you. That would be wonderful. You and James are welcome to stay…if you'd like to spend more time with Nathan."

Grace's smile softened. "I'd like that very much. James would, too."

Ethan's dad was helping him to fortify the ranch. She didn't know if Ethan had called him or if the retired sheriff had just known, with a father's intuition, his son needed him. Either way, James and Grace had arrived without warning. After meeting

Nathan, James had left the house to find his son, and Grace had remained, playing on the floor with Nathan.

Emotion lodged tight in Sienna's throat. "What if Nathan hates me for not telling him sooner?"

Grace reached out, laying her hand over Sienna's. "He deserves the truth—from *you*. He's still young enough that the idea of a dad is exciting. He won't hate you, Sienna. From what I've seen, he already hero-worships Ethan." Grace's voice gentled. "When you tell him Ethan is his father, I think it will be the greatest gift you could give him. I can see he loves Ethan. Tell him, and trust God with the rest."

Sienna drew a shaky breath, letting Grace's wisdom settle deep. She covered Grace's hand with hers. "I will...soon."

Ethan adjusted the angle on the last security camera and stepped back, checking the sight lines across the newly reinforced drive. The ranch looked different now—less like home, more like a fortress.

He dropped the screwdriver into the toolbox and scanned the perimeter beyond the scorched gravel—a grim reminder of his patrol truck going up in flames.

No movement. No signs of anything unusual. Still, unease crawled under his skin.

Wiping his palms on his jeans, he turned toward the barn. His dad had been out there for the past hour, reinforcing the old side doors where the latch had worn loose over the winter. Typical James Callahan. Still showing up when it mattered most.

Ethan spotted him by the fence, crouched low over a new section of bracing, work gloves tucked into his back pocket.

Ethan grabbed his toolbox and headed that way, boots kicking up dust, the Montana sky stretching wide and bruised above him.

"Fence'll hold through a hurricane now." James's focus remained on securing the new bracing, and his voice carried the easy authority Ethan knew so well. His dad had been retired for four years since stepping down after a career that had left his name woven into the history of Hope Haven. James Callahan hadn't just worn the badge—he'd defined what it meant for a generation.

Ethan had earned his own star in the election that followed, not because of the Callahan name, but because he'd spent years proving he could live up to it. He came from a long line of lawmen. Men who believed justice was more than enforcing the law. It was about protecting those who couldn't protect themselves.

His dad hadn't campaigned for him, hadn't endorsed him. Ethan hadn't wanted him to. He'd built his own reputation, following the example his father had set.

Now it was his turn to defend the legacy they'd built. And the people he loved most.

James straightened, dusted off his hands and grinned. "Smells like dinner is about ready."

The rich aroma of beef stew and buttery herbed biscuits wafted on the air, making Ethan's stomach growl in appreciation. "Smells like it. Ready to call it a day?"

"Sure am, son." James collected the toolbox beside his feet. "Wouldn't be able to concentrate with my stomach hankering for good food anyway."

Ethan looked back at the house—the soft glow of the kitchen light, the silhouettes moving inside—and a familiar ache settled in his chest. He wanted to believe things could be this simple again. But part of him still waited for the other shoe to drop. To wake one morning and find Sienna gone. No note. Just another disappearing act.

James glanced at the house, then back at Ethan as they headed round back to the mudroom. "You think she'll stay this time?"

He should've known his astute father would broach the topic. He shrugged. "She hasn't said."

His father studied him a moment longer, then simply nodded. "Have you asked her to stay?"

"I asked if she was leaving when this was over. She said she didn't know."

His dad grunted—half laugh, half breath. "You asked her if she was leaving when this is over?" He shook his head, gave a low chuckle. "No wonder she said she didn't know."

Ethan drew his brows together. What was he missing? "What do you mean?"

James clomped along beside him, stride unhurried. "Give her a reason to stay, son. Don't just stand behind your walls and wait." His dad gave him a hard look as he clapped him on the shoulder. "Not unless you don't mind losing her again."

Ethan swallowed. Walls were all he had left. They'd been his only protection for six years. He'd nearly died once for loving her. Losing her without explanation had carved something deeper than the through-and-through bullet in his back. It had killed his trust—in her, in God, in himself. He wanted to take his father's advice and ask Sienna to stay. He really did.

But a relentless question whispered in the back of his mind: Could he trust her not to vanish again?

Because loving her had never been the problem.

Trusting her not to run. That was the part he hadn't figured out how to do.

TWELVE

"Hi, y'all. I'm Jolene Harper, Mason's office manager." She jogged down the steps of the Blake Ranch office, wiping her hands on the thighs of her jeans as she crossed the yard toward them. Her denim jacket was dusty from the day's work, and a pencil stuck out from her hair on one side.

Sienna gave her a quick smile as she approached. "Uncle Mason said we could come by today."

Jolene returned the smile with a friendly grin. "Mason's real sorry he couldn't be here." She gestured for them to follow. "He had to leave for an urgent meeting and asked me to show you where your daddy's papers are stowed."

A pang of disappointment tugged at Sienna as she fell into step beside Ethan, following Jolene toward the barn. She'd been looking forward to seeing Uncle Mason. Not only because she missed him, but also because part of her had hoped he might help them make sense of everything. But Mason was gone, and even with Nathan safe at Ethan's ranch with Grace and James, the weight of what they might uncover pressed heavy on her chest.

Inside the barn, Jolene paused just past the threshold and swept her hand toward the loft. "You'll find what you're looking for up there."

"Thanks." She and Ethan spoke together.

"No worries, take your time." Jolene stepped outside, then turned back to them. "If you need anything, just holler."

Sienna nodded. "Thanks." She drew a slow, steady breath and took in the cavernous space as Jolene headed back to the office, her boots crunching across the gravel.

The barn smelled of warm hay, wood, dust and the lingering earthy tang of horses and cattle—just as she remembered—yet somehow the memory didn't fit quite right anymore. Across the far wall, a triple stack of hay bales caught flecks of sunlight from the high windows. Everything about the Blake Ranch was cleaner now, more polished, more prosperous. Uncle Mason had taken her father's ranch and turned it into something more.

Ethan scanned the barn with a sheriff's calm attention before nodding toward the ladder. "You ready?"

"As I'll ever be." She blew out a breath and let her gaze climb the ladder leading up to the loft. The wood looked as worn and weathered as she remembered, its rungs smooth from decades of hands and boots. She hadn't set foot up there since her early twenties. A dozen memories crowded her at once. Long summer evenings stacking hay, hiding from chores as a child, and then later, sneaking up here with Ethan, the two of them stealing time away from the world—talking, laughing…dreaming about a future that had once felt so sure.

Her throat tightened. That was all a lifetime ago.

She blinked away an errant tear and forced herself forward.

Ethan stayed back, giving her space, but she could feel his steady gaze following her every move.

The first rung creaked, the sound echoing faintly through the warm, dusty air. She climbed carefully. When she swung herself up into the loft, dust swirled around her boots. Only when she was clear did Ethan follow, his boots thudding against the old wood as he pulled himself up behind her.

The loft creaked under their combined weight, the old boards flexing just enough to make Sienna's breath catch. She scanned the loft. Sunbeams carved shafts of light through the dust-moted air, stirring in lazy spirals where they pierced the gaps between the rafters.

The boxes Mason had promised were piled against the far wall. A haphazard stack of battered cardboard and dented storage bins. Some sagged under their own weight, their sides bowed and splitting; others were sealed tight with strips of sun-bleached packing tape.

She moved toward them, the suspended floor groaning beneath her steps.

Behind her, Ethan shifted, his boots scuffing lightly as he followed, quiet but alert. Always alert.

The closer she got to the boxes, the heavier the air seemed to grow. Not from dust or heat, but from the gravity of what might be buried inside.

She knelt by the nearest box and brushed off a layer of grime with the side of her hand. The faded writing scrawled across the top read: *Blake Ranch: Financials '13–'15.*

Her chest tightened. What would she find in these boxes?

"You okay?" Ethan's voice was low, pitched with concern.

She nodded but kept her attention on the box as she lifted the lid, wincing as the brittle cardboard cracked and gave way. Inside, yellowed papers shifted—invoices, ledger books, tax statements.

She glanced at Ethan. "We need to find the breeding records, evidence of fraud."

Ethan crouched beside her, scanning the other boxes with a critical eye.

"I don't see any labeled like that."

Sienna gave him a sideways glance, catching the smirk playing at the corners of his mouth.

She nudged him with her elbow. "I'm not suggesting we look for a box labeled 'Evidence of Fraud.'"

He chuckled, which made her smile.

Sienna scanned the boxes, her hand brushing away dust so

she could read the faded labels. *Feed Invoices, 1989–1990.* Not what she was looking for.

She peeled the lid back on one of the boxes that had no label, coughing as a new cloud of dust puffed up. Rows of yellowed receipts and supplier bills slumped inside, smelling faintly of old paper and mold.

Behind her, Ethan crouched beside another box and pried it open with a low grunt.

"More feed bills, fertilizer orders and hay delivery receipts." He closed it.

Sienna sifted through a few sheets, her fingers skimming paper, but nothing in the box was helpful. She shook her head and moved to the next box.

Breeding logs. Vet appointments for routine vaccinations. Nothing irregular. Nothing that screamed fraud. She worked her way down the line, the heat in the loft thick against her skin. Dust clung to her, and the rough wood beneath her jeans prickled through the fabric.

The minutes stretched, punctuated only by the occasional creak of a board or the soft rasp of paper. Then her fingers brushed across a folder. A manila file labeled *Registered Lineage, 2017.*

It was empty.

Frowning, she flipped it open and found only a thin layer of dust coating the bottom. No birth certificates, sale agreements or bloodline charts.

Her stomach tightened.

"Ethan." She held up the empty folder.

He glanced up from the papers he was reading. He took the file from her, fanning it open with a scowl. "It was empty?"

"Yeah. It should've contained registered lineage documents. They're gone."

He scanned the shelves around them. "Could it be an oversight? Mason could've kept them in the office rather than stow them out here."

"I guess so." She reached for the next box in the stack. This folder contained a few crumpled invoices. One torn shipping receipt. But there were no records of horse purchases or signed certifications.

"This isn't right. Look." She turned the folder for Ethan to see. "It says, 'Record of Horse Purchase.' But that's not what's inside."

Ethan shifted beside her, the wood creaking under his weight. "Someone could have forgotten to file this stuff."

She dropped the folder back into the box. "You're probably right." She moved to the next box. "Or the papers could have fallen out."

Sienna worked methodically through the nearest stack, wiping dust from brittle folders, scanning each label with growing frustration. Shipping manifests. Veterinary bills. Feed orders. Nothing tied to breeding records or fraud. She shoved aside a cracked bin lid and tugged free a battered accordion file. A folded letter slid loose and dropped to the floor at her knees.

Frowning, she picked it up. The paper was thin, crisp with age. Across the top, the letterhead of Hope Haven Family Medicine stamped in faded blue ink.

Dear Mr. Blake,

Following your annual exam, tests suggest that you have developed coronary artery disease. I'm prescribing Cardiovex, a beta-blocker, to help manage your condition and reduce cardiac strain. Please contact my office if you experience any side effects or worsening symptoms.
Sincerely,
Dr. Monroe Travis

Sienna's stomach turned over. Her father had been sick. Really sick. And she hadn't known. Guilt stabbed deep, because she hadn't been there to see the signs. She hadn't been there when he died. Hadn't even attended his funeral.

Ethan's hand touched her shoulder. "Si, what is it?" He hadn't called her that in a long time—certainly not since she arrived back in Hope Haven. Hearing the nickname now brought fresh tears to her eyes.

She swallowed the rising knot in her throat—grief for her father and for the life she'd lost with Ethan. "It's a letter from my dad's doctor. He had heart disease, and I didn't know."

Ethan gently squeezed her shoulder. "I'm sorry."

"So am I." Carefully, she slipped the letter back into the file. She couldn't let herself dissolve in grief. She had to find the truth, even if it uncovered her father's crime.

At the very bottom of the file, crammed between old tax forms, she found a sealed manila envelope marked *Private— Blake, Jacob.*

Her pulse thundered in her ears as she tore the envelope open. Inside, she found a copy of her father's autopsy report. The words blurred as the evidence of her father's death opened before her. She blinked hard and forced herself to focus.

"I've found my dad's autopsy." She stared at the page as Ethan leaned closer, looking over her shoulder, and then she read, "Cause of death: acute cardiac arrest. Toxicology findings revealed elevated levels of Cardiovex, the prescribed beta-blocker." She speed-read the rest. "It says the levels are consistent with accidental or deliberate overdose." The air was too thick. Too heavy. As if the loft itself pressed down on her. "What do you think this means, Ethan?"

He rubbed the back of his neck. "Do you think your father could have…?"

She was glad he didn't say the words.

"No." She shook her head, unable to comprehend that her dad would do something like that. "He wouldn't have."

Ethan rolled his left shoulder as though it ached. "The level of Cardiovex in his system was elevated. Either he overdosed—whether deliberately or accidentally—or someone else is responsible."

Sienna clasped the letter between her hands. Each new day seemed to bring more questions and less answers. "We have no way of proving either of them."

Her hands shook slightly as she tucked the autopsy report back into the battered file. She skimmed the mess of loose papers still scattered inside the box, hoping—praying—for something that would tell her the truth about the bloodline fraud and her father's part in the whole mess.

Her fingers brushed the stiff edge of a thin card tucked deep between the crumpled tax forms, and she tugged it free. It was a photo. The edges were worn, but the image itself was sharp enough to make her breath catch. Four men stood shoulder to shoulder in front of this barn—her father, Grant Miller, Trip Anderson and Jack Carter.

For a moment, all she could do was stare. "Ethan..." She slowly turned the photo to face him.

He reached for it, his brows drawing tight the instant he saw it. She'd hoped she was wrong. That there was another explanation.

But this photo changed everything.

Crouched beside Sienna, Ethan studied the photo. The four men looked comfortable with each other. Arms casually slung over shoulders, grinning like the camera had caught them mid-joke.

Sienna leaned in for a better look at the photo, her breath warm on his hand. The contact was barely there, but it stirred something sharp and familiar. A fleeting warmth that curled around a part of his heart he thought he'd locked away a long time ago. An awareness of her. The kind that still caught him off guard when he least expected it.

She touched the photo. "I didn't know they were that close, did you?"

He watched her, not the photo, for a long beat. Without warning, a memory hit him—sharp and emotive. Sienna, years younger, laughing as she scrambled up the ladder, tossing him a grin over her shoulder. They'd spent so many stolen hours up here, back when love had seemed simple and the future assured. When he was foolish enough to believe forever was a promise they could keep.

He shook the memory off and focused on the photo.

"No." He'd known Carter for over fifteen years. How was it he had no idea these four men were this close?

"Do you think they were working together?"

"I don't know what they were doing." Truthfully, he didn't know what to think anymore. At every turn, it looked like someone was ready to betray him. "But if Trip and Jacob were tied up in a bloodline fraud, we can't assume Jack and Grant are totally innocent." He shook his head. "This isn't proof of guilt, but it sure does raise a few questions." He met Sienna's big hazel eyes. Her long lashes were flecked with dust, and a streak of grime smudged her chin. But she was still the most beautiful woman he had ever met. "We—" He cleared the sudden husk from his voice. "We need to talk to Carter and Grant." He slid the photo into the back pocket of his jeans, stood and offered her his hand.

She slid her hand into his and let him help her to her feet. Her palm was soft, her fingers warm. He should've released her once she was on her feet, but he didn't. Should've kept his walls up. But the way she looked at him—wide-eyed, uncertain and brave—unraveled him the way she always had.

For a beat too long, neither of them moved.

She stared at him, her gaze dropping to his mouth, then

flicking back to his eyes. It was a tiny, telling moment, but it was long enough. Something changed between them, and the air grew thick. The invisible thread between them tightened until it was almost unbearable. He drew her a step closer, not even conscious of the movement. There were so many things he needed to say. Things like *Please don't leave me again.* But the words wouldn't leave his throat.

Her hand tightened in his. The world narrowed to the soft rise of her breath, the way her lashes fluttered, the faint tremor of her fingers still laced with his.

She leaned in. "Ethan, I—"

"Sienna—"

A loud crack split the moment, jerking Ethan's brain back into working order. The loft shifted beneath them, giving him only a split second to react.

"Si, jump!" Keeping ahold of her hand, he tugged her with him. They sprinted across the shifting loft and launched toward the hay bales stacked against the far wall a heartbeat before the loft gave way behind them in a deafening roar of splintering wood, choking dust and boxes exploding across the barn floor.

Ethan twisted, using his body to shield Sienna's as debris rained down around them. The noise filled his head, shook the ground and vibrated his bones. She clung to him, gasping.

Slowly, he pushed upright, coughing against the dust. Beside him, Sienna coughed, too.

"Are you okay?" The familiar ache from his old gunshot wound flared in his left shoulder blade. He gritted his teeth against the pain, supporting his shoulder with his right hand as he stood, getting his footing in the scattered hay as his eyes found Sienna's.

She nodded, breathless, and clasped the hand he offered to help her up. Together, they turned to stare at the space where the loft had been moments ago. It lay in ruins. Nothing left but a shattered mess of beams and floorboards.

"We could have died." Sienna sank her fingers into her hair, her face drained of color. She glanced at him. "Do you think…?"

"That this was no accident?" He moved to the pile of timber that used to be their spot and hunkered down. He didn't know what he was looking for, but he knew the odds of that loft suddenly coming down was slim to nil. And that was when he spotted the broken beam. He reached for it, bringing it close enough to inspect. Right there, beneath the jagged edge was a straight cut. The kind that resulted from an electric saw. Someone had sawed through the beam, and as he inspected further, he noticed the empty holes where supporting nails used to be.

"Yeah, I'd say this was deliberate." He met Sienna's horrified gaze. "I told Jack we would be at the Blake Ranch today."

She stared at him, stunned. It was clear she didn't want to believe it.

But the evidence said otherwise.

THIRTEEN

Ethan pulled his newly assigned patrol SUV into the Hope Haven Sheriff's Department lot, climbed out and headed inside to question Carter about the photo he and Sienna had found in Jacob Blake's papers.

After the loft collapsed onto the barn floor, Jolene and a few ranch hands had hurried to the scene. What followed had been chaotic and had forced Ethan to clear everyone out to secure the area. He'd called it in, bagged the sawed-through beam and the posts with missing nails as evidence and assigned his deputies to begin the investigation. There was no doubt in his mind—someone had sabotaged the structure.

Once he got Sienna safely back to the ranch with Nathan and his parents, he'd headed straight here. He had questions for Jack Carter. At the top of his list was Jack's connection to Trip Anderson and Jacob Blake.

Ethan's feet hit the front steps of the station, adrenaline burning up the fatigue in his blood. He pulled open the door, every nerve in his body buzzing with urgency.

The moment he entered the bullpen, his stare landed on Carter sitting at his desk, leafing through papers in a file. The other deputies milled around, sat at desks, queued at the coffeepot or were gathered in front of a board pinned with the latest case evidence.

"Hey, Sheriff," came the greetings as he stalked to Carter's desk. Ethan returned them, his attention never leaving his second-in-command.

Carter raised his head as Ethan stopped in front of him. "Hey, Ethan, what's up?"

"My office." He turned and strode out of the bullpen.

Carter fell into step beside him. "What's going on? Has something happened?"

Ethan entered his office and swung the door shut behind him. He slipped the photo from his back jeans pocket and flipped it around for Carter to see. "You tell me. Is there something I should know?"

Carter squinted at the picture. "What do you mean?"

"When was this taken?"

Carter shrugged. "I don't know. A few years ago, maybe?"

Ethan put the photo on his desk, nailing it to the surface with his index finger. "You look pretty chummy with Trip Anderson and Jacob Blake."

Carter met his stare. "What are you saying?"

"I didn't realize you knew these men so well, given that Trip Anderson lives in Idaho." Ethan folded his arms across his chest, widened his stance. "Both men are tied to the bloodline fraud I'm investigating. Do you know that?"

"What are you saying, Ethan? That I'm guilty by association?" Carter raked his hands through his hair. "Look, Trip is a friend of Jacob Blake. Jacob used to let me and a few friends hunt on his land sometimes. I invited you once but—"

"I don't hunt," Ethan cut in.

"Yeah, that's what you said then, too." Carter began to pace like he was trying to run off bad energy. "Back then, you were still smarting over Sienna and wanted nothing to do with her family. I wasn't even allowed to speak her name, remember?"

"I remember." Had he been that bitter? That unforgiving?

"The photo was taken after one particularly successful hunting weekend. Jacob and Trip were with us."

"Who is 'us'?"

"Me, Rick, Lenny." Carter stopped pacing, snatched the picture off the desk and shoved it beneath Ethan's nose. "If you look closely, there's a bull elk lying in the background." He poked a finger against the picture. "We'd just brought it in when someone snapped the pic."

Ethan let his gaze drop to the photo. He could just about make out a bull elk in the barn, just as Carter had said. "Why are Rick and Lenny not in the photo?"

"I don't know… Lenny took the pic on his phone. Rick was… I don't remember what Rick was doing."

Ethan wanted to believe him, but too many things didn't add up. "Since Sienna arrived, we've had a semitruck try to collide with us head-on, someone broke into the ranch with the intention of murdering Sienna in her bed, my patrol truck blew up just as we were due to leave for the secured cabin in Elk Ridge. Then we were ambushed on the way, and today the barn loft Sienna and I were on collapsed. On each occasion I spoke to you about my plans beforehand." He met Carter's gaze, ticked off his fingers as he continued. "You knew Sienna and Nathan were with me at my ranch. You knew when we were heading to Elk Ridge. And you knew we'd be at the Blake Ranch today."

"Ethan, you can't really think I'm involved in this." The astonishment on Carter's face was pretty convincing. Either the man was a talented actor or he was telling the truth. "You've known me for years. I'd die before I put Sienna or her child in danger. Before I put *you* in danger."

"Then explain how these people always seem to be one step ahead of us, Jack."

"I *didn't* tell anyone." Carter's voice dropped. "The only way that information got shared out of my mouth is if someone was eavesdropping."

Something in Carter's voice gave Ethan pause. Not just the

sincerity, but the certainty. *The only way that information got shared was if someone was eavesdropping.*

What if Carter was telling the truth? And he hadn't deliberately shared the information. "Have you checked the camera feed?"

Carter dropped into one of the blue fabric chairs in front of Ethan's desk. "I played it back three times. No one was anywhere near me when we spoke about the cabin in Elk Ridge."

He let everything Carter said sink in. Let the jumble of thoughts, questions and logical conclusions mull around in his brain. Until one possible explanation came to mind. He stared at Carter, seeing not the man who had possibly betrayed him but his friend—a man who might very well be innocent.

"What if your phone's compromised?" The skin on the back of Ethan's neck went cold. "Hacked. Cloned. Something."

The blood drained from Carter's face. "You think someone's been listening in?"

"It'd certainly explain a few things. If someone hacked your phone, they'd have access to your messages, your calls, everything you do."

For a long beat, Carter remained motionless. Then he jumped to his feet, pulled out his phone and stared at it like it had morphed into a prairie rattlesnake. He raised his gaze to Ethan's. "Maybe *your* phone is the one they hacked."

"Yeah, I thought of that, too." He unfolded his arms. "Let's go see Dustin. I want a forensic scan run on our phones. And while we're there, I'll get him to pull the data from the self-driving semi. If they got to our phones, they might've gotten to that truck, too."

Carter blinked. "You think the semi was hacked?"

"It's a real possibility."

Dustin, the department's tech specialist, was hunched over a cluttered workstation in the IT room when they stepped inside.

He looked up, blinking behind wire-rimmed glasses perched low on his nose.

"Sheriff Callahan, how can I help?" He sat up and rubbed his hands together.

Ethan held out his phone, and Carter followed suit. "We need a full forensic sweep on these. They might be compromised."

Dustin took the phones and hooked them up to a small device. "If there's a compromise, we'll find it in a few minutes." Lights flickered across the scanner as he tapped in a few commands.

The room filled with the quiet hum of cooling fans and the rapid clicking of Dustin's keyboard. Carter stood with his hands stuffed in his pockets. Ethan stayed at Dustin's side, watching the data scroll across the computer screen.

Ethan nodded toward the server bay. "Did the recovery team bring in the black box from the semi?"

Dustin shook his head. "Not yet."

"When it arrives, make it your top priority to find out if it was hacked."

"Copy that." Dustin leaned closer to the monitor, brows pinched as he stared at the data. "Okay. Found something."

Ethan stared at the screen over Dustin's shoulder, having no clue what all the information meant. "What did you find?"

"Your phone is clean, Sheriff." He unplugged the phone and handed it to Ethan. "But Carter's phone was cloned." Dustin's fingers moved rapidly over the keyboard. "The phone's data stream was intercepted. Someone had real-time access to calls and messages. Possibly even audio."

Carter's mouth dropped open as he turned his stunned gaze to Ethan. "*That's* how they knew where you were going."

A chill slid between Ethan's shoulder blades, his mind running through every phone conversation he'd had with Carter. Every plan he'd made since the night Sienna returned had been exposed. It wasn't hard for the enemy to stay one step ahead of them when they knew his every move.

"Mommy?" Under Sienna's supervision, Nathan pushed his hands into the arms of his Toy Story pajama top and pulled it down.

"Yes, peanut." She kept her tone light, even though her stomach had been in knots all evening. Ethan had left hours ago to meet with Carter and Grant, and when he still hadn't returned, she'd tried calling, but it had gone to voicemail. His parents had offered to stay until he got back, but she'd assured them she'd be fine—even though she always felt safer when Ethan was close. The ranch was secure now: extra locks, cameras, new alarms. But that hadn't stopped her from checking every door and window three times and keeping an anxious eye on the security monitor in Ethan's home office. She'd done her best to stay calm for Nathan's sake, had prayed protection over them, but a tight knot of worry banded her chest.

Nathan's soft voice pulled her back. "Mommy?"

"Yes, baby?" She kissed her sweet boy's head. Getting him ready for bed had always been one of her favorite times of the day.

He gazed up at her with his most serious expression. "I was thinking."

"Yeah?" She pulled back the covers on the bed they shared and sat on the edge. There were enough spare rooms at the ranch for Nathan to have his own, but she wanted him to be with her to protect him.

"Yeah." He placed Woody on his pillow. "I was having a big think."

"Wow. A *big* think?" She tapped a gentle finger on the tip of his nose. It was the one feature he had of hers. "What were you thinking about?"

"I was thinking that if we stayed here, Sheriff Callahan could be my dad."

His words punched the breath from her lungs. She knew he looked up to Ethan, but she never guessed he might look to him as a father. An ache pressed into her chest. Had her son been so deprived of a male role model that he latched onto the first one to come along? Or did he somehow, deep down, sense that Ethan was more than the sheriff who was helping them? A kind of primordial recognition? She couldn't deny the instant bond Nathan and Ethan had, or how much her son needed his father.

Her fear of the possible emotional fallout had kept her from telling him. For so long, it had been just the two of them. What if he stopped loving her because she kept Ethan from him? *Please, Father, don't let him hate me.*

She stroked her hand over his head. His hair was soft beneath her palm and his gaze was so hopeful, it twinged her heart and made her throat sting. Nathan's hope and innocence were the two things she most feared wounding. Ethan hadn't indicated that he wanted her to stay. Not once since she arrived. In fact, sometimes she was sure he couldn't wait for her to leave again.

"We can't stay here, peanut. We have our home in Idaho. All your toys and friends are there."

He thought for a moment while Sienna sat with her hands tightly clasped in her lap, desperately praying for God to help her do the right thing.

"I know!" He beamed at her like he'd just come up with the most amazing solution. "Sheriff Callahan can come to Idaho with us."

Her heart panged. That was not what she was expecting. She softened her voice, choosing her words carefully. Nathan's little heart was so tender, the hope in his bright blue eyes pressed a thick lump to the back of her throat. She couldn't do anything to crush that hope.

How could she explain the complicated truth without dimming his innocent light? He'd already been through so much. New places. New dangers. Uncertainty pressing in from every side. His trust and faith in the people he loved was a fragile, precious thing she couldn't bear to shatter.

She reached for his hands, emotion pinching beneath her ribs when his soft grip tightened around hers. "Sheriff Callahan is the sheriff of Hope Haven, sweetheart." She smoothed her thumbs over his knuckles. "He can't just leave. Who would protect the residents of this town?"

His little shoulders drooped. Crestfallen, he lifted tear-filled eyes to her, his bottom lip quivering as he fought to hold back tears. "But I love him, Mommy."

Sienna nearly burst into tears. Why was this so hard? Still, fear of Nathan's anger kept her paralyzed. She pulled him into a hug, her heart aching for him…for all the pain she'd brought to the two most important people in her life.

"It's getting late. How about we talk about this tomorrow?"

Several seconds ticked by before Nathan finally nodded against her shoulder. When he began to wriggle, she released him. "Come on, time for prayers."

He knelt on the plush rug beside the bed and pressed his hands together. Then he glanced at her, and while he'd been brave enough not to let his tears fall, they were still evident in his eyes. Sienna's heart squeezed.

"Can I say the prayers tonight, Mommy?"

"Um…yes…" Usually, she guided him through his bedtime prayers, so his request surprised her. "Sure." She knelt beside him. "Whenever you're ready, baby."

"Dear, Heavenly Father," he began, his voice soft. He cracked open one eye and peeked up at her, seeking approval. This child melted her heart.

She gave him a reassuring smile. "Go on."

He closed his eyes and leaned on his clasped hands. "Thank you for protecting us from the bad man. And thank you for my mommy and Sheriff Callahan. He's really cool. I like him. My daddy had to go away, and I'd really like a daddy. Please…can you make Sheriff Callahan my daddy? I don't mind if we have to stay here. I can make new friends. Thank you very much. Hallelujah! Amen."

A sharp ache flared in Sienna's chest, her breath catching on her whispered, "Amen." She brushed a kiss to his temple, squeezing her eyes shut against the sting of tears.

She helped him climb into bed. "Mommy, do you think He heard?"

Sienna pulled the blanket snug over him. "God always hears your prayers, sweetheart." Her voice wobbled, but Nathan didn't seem to notice.

He looked up at her with sleepy eyes, opening his arms for a hug. "Okay. Night-night, Mommy."

"Good night, baby. Sweet dreams." It was all Sienna could do to hold it together as she tucked him in. Her throat closed, guilt and fear rising so thick they stole her breath.

His breathing evened out. He was already slipping toward sleep. She brushed her hand over his hair, her throat aching. Torn between the need to preserve her relationship with her son and the fear that, like Ethan, he wouldn't be able to forgive her, she'd delayed telling Nathan the truth. She'd promised Grace she'd tell Nathan that Ethan was his father. And tonight had made one thing heartbreakingly clear: no matter how scared she was, she couldn't put it off anymore.

She remained sitting on the bed next to Nathan a moment longer, her heart heavy and aching, before rising quietly so as not to disturb him. She turned and her breath hitched.

Ethan stood in the doorway, shadowed by the soft glow of the dimmed hall light, his palm pressed against the doorframe. She hadn't even heard him come in. His throat worked, but he didn't speak. His eyes locked with hers, unreadable but piercing, and something in her belly twisted tight.

He'd heard.

She saw it in his eyes, in his stunned stillness. But how much had he heard?

Sienna stared at him, exhaustion and something raw in her eyes, but it was the tears clinging to her lashes that punched him hardest. She swiped them away, straightened her shoulders and somehow still looked so incredibly vulnerable. All he wanted was to hold her, to reassure her. But…reassure her of what? She'd kept the truth from their son for a reason. Was she afraid he wouldn't be a good enough father?

He lingered in the doorway, Nathan's words looping through his mind: *Please…can you make Sheriff Callahan my daddy? I don't mind if we have to stay here. I can make new friends.* And before that—*But I love him, Mommy.* The simple, innocent declaration had hit harder than anything else, wrapping around his heart like Nathan's little hands and squeezing, filling him with a strange mix of pain and joy unlike anything he'd ever known. Ethan had fallen hard for his son the moment Sienna had shown up at his office, Nathan's small hand tucked securely in hers. Ethan hadn't understood that fierce protective instinct that kicked in the second he met the little boy, but he did now. Nathan loved him…without even knowing he was his father. And that undid him in ways he couldn't begin to explain.

His father's advice came back to him. *Give her a reason to stay, son. Don't just stand behind your walls and wait. Not unless you don't mind losing her again.* And the third strike came in Jack Carter's voice: *Back then, you were still smarting over Sienna and wanted nothing to do with her family. I wasn't even allowed to speak her name, remember?*

For too long he'd let bitterness rule him. He still wasn't sure he could forgive her, but he could certainly try to move forward. Be the father Nathan deserved. He could ask her to move back to Hope Haven so they could co-parent their son.

Sienna tiptoed from the room. "I didn't hear you come back."

He straightened, dropping his hand from the doorframe, his voice low. "Just got in."

She pulled the door to a crack behind her, shoulders held taut, as though steeling herself for whatever came next. Her eyes searched his, still shining a little too brightly in the dim hallway.

"Everything okay? Did you talk to Grant and Carter?" She pointed down the hall, indicating that they should take the conversation to the front room.

His gaze flicked over her. She looked exhausted—tired eyes and golden-brown hair pulled back in a ponytail that left tendrils framing her face. Not in an artful arrangement, more like a progression of curls that had gradually escaped the elastic band. She hadn't changed for bed yet, still in jeans and a light sweater, like she'd been waiting up. For him? Or just too keyed up to settle?

He strolled with her to the family room and dropped onto the couch. To his surprise, she sat beside him.

"I spoke to Carter. Grant is off fishing for the next few days." He scrubbed a hand over his face, the weight of the day sinking deeper now that he was at home. So, they were doing this? Ignoring what he'd just overheard? Okay, if she wanted to play it that way, he'd go along for now. "Turns out, Carter and some friends were hunting with Jacob and Trip the weekend the picture was taken. Jacob used to let them hunt on his land. The picture was taken after a hunt that won them a bull elk, which can be seen in the background." He heaved in a breath. He needed to bring her up to speed, but he also wanted nothing more than to address the topic they were skirting. "The photo was innocent and so is Carter. He wasn't sharing our plans with the enemy. They cloned his phone. We found out today when our tech specialist uncovered the cloning attack."

Sienna covered her mouth with both hands. "You're kidding."

He shook his head. The disbelief in her eyes mirrored his

own when he'd first learned the truth. If Carter hadn't been so adamant, his thoughts might never have run to the possibility of phone hacking. "I only wish I was."

"What did you do when you found out?" The way the soft glow of the lamp caught the curve of her cheek made it hard to look away.

"Dustin—our tech guy—scrubbed Carter's phone and installed extra security in both our phones to prevent any future attacks. I think it might be prudent to do the same with yours. Don't use it until Dustin has a chance to review it."

"Okay…" She stared into the middle distance, worrying the cuff of her sweater sleeve as though she couldn't quite comprehend the enormity of what he'd just told her. She turned back to him. "Did you say Trip and my dad were hunting with them?" Her brows pinched, creating a cute little furrow between them. Ethan glanced away. He shouldn't be thinking about how cute anything was on her. "I didn't know Trip knew my dad."

"According to Jack, they were friends."

Sienna nibbled on her thumbnail. "I always thought it strange that Trip headhunted me just when I needed a job…just after I got to Idaho." She gave Ethan a sideways glance as though cautious of the subject. As if it might trigger him or something.

He dragged a hand over his jaw. "I would surmise that Jacob had something to do with the job offer."

Sienna rubbed her thumb over the edge of her opposite thumbnail, her gaze fixed on the small motion. "I'm not sure whether he was looking out for me and trying to protect me… or if he was using Trip to keep an eye on me. To make sure I didn't talk."

"I guess we'll never know now."

"I guess not." Her gaze flicked toward the hall behind her, her voice faltering. "How much of that did you hear?"

Ahh, so not avoiding, just postponing. "I heard Nathan praying for me to be his dad."

"Oh…" She bit her bottom lip.

"Yes, *oh*." He sat forward, bracing his forearms on his knees and locking his fingers.

She curled her bare toes into the rug beneath their feet—a textured rustic his mom had insisted would bring warmth to the room. "I'm going to tell him."

He stared at her, holding her gaze, one eyebrow cocked.

She shifted and hugged her arms around her middle. "I *am*."

"I didn't say anything."

Her smile flickered—brief, tight—but it lit up her face for that one fleeting moment. "You didn't have to. Your interrogation eyebrow did it for you."

He had an interrogation eyebrow? That pulled a twitch from the corner of his mouth, easing the tension between them just a fraction.

"I want to be Nathan's dad. I *am* Nathan's dad, and I deserve to be part of his life. He deserves to have his father around every day from now on."

Her gaze dipped, lashes casting faint shadows on her cheeks. "I know."

"Then why did you tell him your life was in Idaho?" He kept his tone calm, but the hurt of hearing her say it still left a dull ache.

She winced. "You heard that?"

"Assume I pretty much heard everything."

She sucked in a breath. "Ethan, I—I…" Her words faltered, her shoulders sagging.

"He deserves the truth." He met her gaze squarely. "We both know that."

She nodded, chewing on her bottom lip. "I know." When she raised her gaze to meet his, her eyes were filled with tears again. Her lips trembled. "I'm scared he's going to hate me when I tell him the truth."

Ethan held up his hand, wanting to comfort her, but he was

afraid that if he touched her, he'd pull her into his arms, and he'd lose his heart to her all over again. He'd almost kissed her in the barn loft today; he wasn't sure he had the willpower to resist her again. He patted her awkwardly on the shoulder, which somehow made her laugh…and cry at the same time. The delicate sound twisted his insides, and something far more dangerous crept in at the edges.

Ethan was so far out of his depth that he didn't know what to do. All he could think to say was, "He won't hate you, Si. I won't let that happen."

"Don't call me that." Her voice dropped, her gaze sliding away as though she couldn't bear to look at him.

He searched her face. "What? Si?" He hadn't called her by the nickname in what felt like forever, but after it slipped out today in the barn loft, it suddenly became natural to call her by the name he'd used all those years ago.

"Yes…it fools me into thinking we're okay." Her voice thinned to almost a whisper. "That you've forgiven me."

The ache in her tone made him want to fix the brokenness between them.

"I'm trying. I really am." He stared down at his hands, fingers locked so tight his knuckles had gone white. "I searched for you."

She blinked, surprise flickering across her face. "You did?"

"It was about seven months after you left. I'd been beside myself for months thinking that something happened to you, then I found you in Idaho, working for Trip Anderson."

She stilled, as if he'd caught her off guard. "You found me? So, you knew I was pregnant?" She scrambled to her feet. "And you didn't come for me?"

"I didn't know you were pregnant."

Sienna stared at him like she thought he was kidding. "How could you not have known? I was eight months *pregnant*. That isn't usually easy to miss."

"You were working with a horse and a teenage girl was with you. You were laughing. I watched you for a while, wanting to go to you, to confront you, but in the end, I decided I was too angry to hear anything you had to say. I wouldn't have been able to listen to whatever excuse you gave at the time, so I left."

She reared back, her whole stance conveying astonishment. "You knew I was pregnant and that it could only be with your child, and you walked away?"

"Your back was turned to me the whole time. I never saw your belly. From behind, you didn't look pregnant, Sienna. If I'd noticed you were carrying my child, I would never have left you to raise him alone."

She walked over to the window, leaned against the frame. "All this time, you knew where I was…" Her words were softly spoken, yet they pierced him deeper than if she'd screamed them at him.

Physically, only the room separated them, but emotionally, an entire continent had opened between them. Trying to remove the distance, he pushed off the couch and went to stand at the window with her.

"I'm sorry." He pulled her into his arms and hugged her, relieved when she came willingly. She didn't hug him back, but she did rest her head against his chest and let him hug her.

"You really didn't know I was pregnant?"

"I would've *never* walked away if I'd known."

"Then I forgive you."

Her words landed a heavy blow to his heart. He'd seen the hurt in her eyes when she thought he'd deliberately abandoned her to go through the pregnancy alone, yet she'd been quick to forgive him. Why couldn't he bring himself to do the same for her? He drew in a breath, then slowly released it. No matter how hard he tried, he wasn't ready to take that step. Forgiveness meant opening his heart again. He'd trusted her with his heart once, and she shattered it the day she left.

She turned her head, laying her cheek against his chest. "I'm sorry I left you. I would've never done that if your life hadn't been so viciously threatened. I wanted a life with you, Ethan. I wanted to be your wife."

That kicked him in the gut harder than an unprovoked kick from a mule. Stupidly, his throat tightened, stealing his ability to reply, not that he actually knew what to say. *Thank you* would've been a ridiculous response. So he hugged her tighter, and something loosened in his chest when she hugged him back.

"Stay." He said the word so quietly, she couldn't have heard him. He cleared his throat and tried again. "Stay in Hope Haven and let's co-parent Nathan."

She leaned her head back, looking at him with such hope, it humbled him. "You want me to stay?"

"Yes…it'll make co-parenting easier. I don't want to be an every-other-weekend dad. I want to be hands-on right from the start."

She stiffened, pushing out of his embrace. His brows drew together. What had he said? Her lips pressed tight, shoulders rising, and a flicker of wariness lit the depths of her liquid amber-green eyes. Not anger. Not hurt, exactly. Disappointment? His muscles tensed. He'd meant to offer something solid, something *reassuring*, but suddenly it looked like he'd messed up—again.

"You want me to stay so we can co-parent Nathan?"

He nodded. "Exactly."

She watched him closely. "And that's the only reason?"

Why did he sense he was being tested? A prickle worked its way down his spine. Not the kind that warned of danger. This was something else. Something fragile.

"What other reason would there be?"

Her shoulders sagged. She sighed, gaze dropping, like she'd just accepted some unspoken truth.

"Okay, I'll stay for Nathan's sake." She turned away, and he gently caught her wrist, halting her.

"What did I say to upset you?"

She shrugged. "Nothing. You didn't say anything I hadn't already expected."

"What does that mean?"

She shook her head. "Forget it, Ethan. You asked me to stay for Nathan, and I love my son too much to hurt him by leaving. So I'll stay."

Confusion tightened his chest. "Are you saying you don't want to stay?"

"Once we tell Nathan you're his father, there really is no other option." She eased her wrist out of his light clasp. "Good night, Ethan."

But he couldn't let her go, not when he wished he knew the right words to take the anguish out of her eyes.

"Sienna, wait." He caught her. "We can figure this out together."

She turned slowly, stared at him, tears brimming again, her free hand pressed to her chest like she was holding herself together. She opened her mouth, closed it, then shook her head sadly and whispered, "Ethan…" Whatever words followed, they seemed to get caught in her throat.

He didn't know exactly what he'd done, only that somehow, he'd hurt her—and strangely enough, it hurt him, too. Heart thudding with a quiet, fierce hope he hadn't let himself feel in years, he drew her to him. Unable to help himself, he kissed her.

And finally, the first crack appeared in the wall they'd both been hiding behind.

FOURTEEN

Lord, thank You for bringing us safely through the night. Please give me courage for today.

Sienna lay in the hush of morning, watching the early Montana dawn filter through the soft cotton curtains and cast a pale wash of light across the room. Beside her, Nathan was gradually waking. She drew in a fortifying breath and exhaled slowly. It was time to tell him. She couldn't leave it any longer.

Last night, Ethan had asked her to stay. Not because he wanted to rebuild what they'd lost. It was because he wanted to be a father to his son.

And why shouldn't he? She had no right to expect more, not after the way she'd left, the hurt she'd caused. But part of her—the foolish, hopeful part—still wondered if the kiss they'd shared had meant anything. For a few brief seconds, she'd let herself fall into the kiss, believing they could be more. She'd lost herself in his warmth, his strength, the memory of what they used to be.

But then he'd pulled back, murmured something about needing to get some sleep and put the width of the room between them.

Trying not to feel rejected, she'd nodded, slipped away to the guest room and spent half the night staring at the ceiling, wondering if they'd ever be Ethan and Sienna again. She pushed the thought away. This wasn't about her; it was about their son.

Whatever lay ahead, Nathan was who mattered. His happiness. His comfort. His future. Even if it meant anchoring herself here in Hope Haven, building a life alongside Ethan without ever being allowed back inside his heart.

She wanted to believe she could stay just for Nathan's sake. That she could put her hurt aside and be strong, practical. But would her heart survive living in the same town, the same orbit, the same world as Ethan Callahan…without ever regaining the part of him she'd lost?

Would she be strong enough to live like that? To watch him be the father Nathan needed without aching for the man she still loved? She suspected every day would be a living heartbreak, but she'd do it for Nathan. He was her priority. She had to accept that whatever she and Ethan once had was over. Closing her eyes, she looked inward. *Lord, help me to stop dwelling on what might have been. Help me to focus on what matters now.*

Jack wasn't the mole. That was something to be grateful for.

He was more than Ethan's deputy; he was his friend. Someone Ethan had trusted for years. If he'd been the one feeding information to the people trying to kill her, it would have been another betrayal Ethan didn't deserve. He already carried the heartbreak of what she'd done. She saw it every time he looked at her, every time his guard slipped just enough to let the pain show through. If he'd had to face the betrayal of his closest friend, too—someone who'd stood beside him since their teenage years—it would have crushed him.

The cloned phone explained how the enemy always stayed one step ahead. But it didn't bring them any closer to knowing who was behind the bloodline fraud or who was so determined to erase her. Nathan stirred, coming fully awake. She watched him, her heart warming when he turned sleep-fogged eyes to her. For so long it had been just the two of them.

"Morning, Mommy." He blinked up at her, his voice still sleepy as he sat up.

She smiled, smoothing his bed hair. "Morning, sweet boy."

He yawned, face scrunching as he scratched his head. "What day is it?"

"Sunday." She threw back the covers. Since they were both awake, she might as well get them ready for the day.

"Are we going to church?"

"Not today." She hated missing church, but it might be better to stay close to the ranch where they were safe. There was no telling how far her pursuers would go, and she didn't want to risk other people getting hurt.

Nathan's eyes suddenly lit up, and he gave her a wide grin. "Happy Mother's Day!"

Sienna blinked, surprised he remembered. Warmth flooded her chest. "Thank you, sweetheart."

Nathan threw his small arms around her neck, and she hugged him to her. "Sheriff Callahan told me not to forget. He said Sunday is Mother's Day, and I should tell you Happy Mother's Day first thing because you're the best mommy in the world."

Her throat tightened, tears pricking her eyes as she hugged him, kissing the side of his head. Something about the small gesture of reminding their son to wish her a happy Mother's Day touched her deeply. "He said that?"

Nathan wriggled out of the hug, nodding. "He said you're really brave, too."

A laugh slipped from her, even if it was watery. Her sweet boy had prayed for the father he had all along. No matter the consequences of her actions, he deserved to know his father was just down the hall. She needed to be brave. One of her favorite Bible verses came to mind. *For God has not given us a spirit of fear, but of power and of love and of a sound mind*—2 Timothy 1:7.

She'd dreaded this moment for so long, afraid the truth would shatter the precious bond she had with her son. She inhaled, then released the breath in a whoosh, both dreading what was to come and strangely excited for her son. Mother's Day was the perfect day to tell Nathan about his father.

"Peanut…" She reached for his hands. "I have something important to tell you…"

She wasn't sure how the words would come, only that God would give her the strength to speak them. All she could do now was hope Nathan would understand. And that when the truth came out, he'd still look at her the same way.

Ethan leaned against the counter, phone pressed to his ear, surrounded by pancake ingredients.

"Mom, do you think God gives second chances?" Ever since last night, he'd been pondering the question. If anyone would have an answer, his mom would. He'd called to wish her a Happy Mother's Day, and somehow the conversation had led here.

"Of course He does. He's a God of second chances. However, I think sometimes He lets us walk through fire so we recognize the gift when it returns." Her soft words resonated deep inside him.

He certainly felt as though he'd been walking through fire since Sienna left Hope Haven, and the heat hadn't eased when she returned. She'd agreed to stay, but he sensed if she felt she had a choice, she wouldn't have agreed to move back to town.

"Are you asking about second chances because of Sienna?" His mom's gentle question cracked right into the truth he hadn't wanted to voice. He should've known her wisdom wouldn't let him get this past her.

Propping against the counter, he crossed one ankle over the other. "Yeah… I've been thinking about it." His voice dropped. "But I don't know how to forgive her, Mom. She took everything I thought we had and just…walked away."

For a moment, Grace was quiet on the other end of the line.

Then her voice came with that soft motherly tone he knew so well. "You can carry that hurt for the rest of your life, Ethan, but the thing about hurt feelings is that they'll always stop you from fully seeing the other person's side."

Warmth crawled up the back of his neck. If he were honest, he'd never looked at this from Sienna's viewpoint.

"You might think you're protecting yourself," his mom continued gently, "but you're also making it harder for her to reach you. She might be here now, but if she starts believing there's no way forward for the two of you…she'll stop trying, honey. She'll guard her heart, and in time it will harden against you."

The words hit like a clean punch, knocking the air out of him. He gripped the phone, the weight of his mom's words settling heavy on his heart.

Sienna had agreed to stay—for Nathan. But if he didn't figure out how to let go of the past, she'd wall herself off for good. And then it wouldn't matter if she was right here in Hope Haven…she'd still be gone.

He poured the flour he'd measured into the mixing bowl and reached for the eggs. His mom had made sure he and his sister, Kelly knew how to cook. He might not often have time in the kitchen, which was why his mom usually came by to make dinner, but he knew his way around ingredients. Right now, he was preparing to make Sienna pancakes. It wasn't much, but it was a chance to share something special with Nathan.

Helping his son make his mom a Mother's Day breakfast— something he and Kelly had loved doing with their dad as kids—would give them bonding time. As much as he wanted to tell Nathan he was his father, he would never undermine Sienna like that. It had to be her call. And when she was ready.

He exhaled, forcing a smile his mom couldn't see. "Thanks, Mom. You always shine a light where I least want to look."

She chuckled softly. "That's what moms are for."

Her words tugged a chuckle from him. "Happy Mother's Day."

"Thank you, sweetheart."

He ended the call, then set the phone down beside the mixing bowl, his palm lingering a moment on the cool countertop as a hollow ache bloomed in his chest. Sienna was staying, but if he didn't find a way to leave the past behind…he risked losing her all over again.

Sienna's pulse thudded. *Please, please don't let him hate me.* "I love you so very much, you know that, right?"

Nathan nodded, giving her his signature eye roll. "I know 'cause you tell me all the time." Then he grinned. "I love you too, Mommy."

IIis assurance tightened the knots in her stomach. She rubbed her thumbs over the backs of his hands, blinking against the sudden sting of emotion.

"The important thing I need to tell you is that Sheriff Callahan—Ethan—is your dad." There was so much she needed to explain, but Nathan was only a child. At this age, he wouldn't understand half of her explanation, and she didn't know how to explain the past without confusing him.

His eyes went wide, his mouth falling open. She couldn't breathe, heart squeezing so tight it almost hurt, bracing for the heartbreak she'd feared for so long.

But then he bounced on the mattress with pure, unfiltered joy. "Really?" He launched upward, throwing his arms around her neck. "Mommy! God did it! He answered my prayer!"

Relief poured through her, so powerful it unleashed the tears she'd been fighting. She hugged him tightly. *Thank You, Lord.*

Nathan pulled back, bouncing with excitement. "I have to tell him!" He scrambled out of bed, and dashed for the door as soon as his little feet hit the floor.

"Peanut, wait!" But Nathan was in full bulldoze mode. By

the time she leaped out of bed and dashed to the door, he'd already bolted past the doorway.

Sienna dropped onto the edge of the bed as her son's excited shout echoed through the ranch.

"Sheriff Callahan's my daddy! Sheriff Callahan's my daddy!"

Ethan didn't have time to brace for the small body that careened into him, arms wrapping around him from behind. He'd heard Nathan's voice ringing through the ranch, "Sheriff Callahan's my daddy!" and barely had time to register the wave of joy and relief before his son shot into the kitchen.

"You're my real daddy." Small arms squeezed around his waist, hugging hard.

Ethan froze for half a breath, a knot lodged under his ribs. Slowly resting his hands on Nathan's narrow shoulders, he eased him backward to give himself room to turn around.

"You're my daddy!" Nathan tipped his head back, grinning wide, eyes bright. "You're my daddy!" His hands patted Ethan's sides as he bounced with excitement. "Mommy told me! I prayed and prayed, and God answered! I knew it!"

Ethan dropped to one knee, bringing himself eye to eye with the boy he'd yearned to claim since he first learned of his existence. He ruffled Nathan's sleep-tousled hair. "Yeah, buddy. I'm your daddy." To his shock, his throat tightened, making his voice rough. "And there's nothing in this world I'll ever love more than you and being your dad."

Nathan practically vibrated with joy, half laughing, half gasping. "Whatcha doing?"

"Waiting for you to help me make pancakes for your mom. It's Mother's Day—"

"I remembered. I told Mommy Happy Mother's Day first thing, like you said."

"Good man." Ethan smiled, a real, full smile that softened the tightness in his chest. He tousled Nathan's hair again and pressed a quick kiss to his son's forehead. "Now go tell Mommy to stay in her room until we call her, okay? This is her surprise."

Nathan gave a wide, exaggerated nod, eyes sparkling. "I'll tell her!" He darted off, feet thudding down the hall, voice already calling out, "Mommy! Stay in your room! It's a surprise!"

Ethan let out a slow breath, steadying himself on the counter with both hands. His chest ached, but for once, it wasn't from anger or hurt. It was something warmer, heavier, stirring deep inside.

He smiled faintly to himself and reached for the whisk. Maybe he'd been holding on too tightly to the past. Maybe it was time to let go.

Nathan clutched her fingers as he eagerly towed her to the kitchen.

"Come on, Mommy. You can't peek yet." His voice pitched high with excitement, Nathan's feet slapped the wooden floor. "Daddy said it's a surprise."

She barely noticed her own steps as Nathan tugged her forward. *Daddy.* For years, she'd braced herself for this moment, imagining the questions, the hurt, the confusion. She'd never pictured this—her son's voice ringing with such unguarded joy. The simplicity of it undid her, softening defenses she hadn't even realized were still in place.

And then the scent hit her. Sweet batter, a whisper of vanilla, the faint toasty edge of pancakes. A small ache bloomed in her chest. Ethan had always been good in the kitchen. He'd show up with groceries, insisting on making her dinner after a long workday, or he'd sometimes drop by early on a Saturday, teasing her into trying his latest pancake recipe. She used to think no one could flip a pancake as perfectly as he did.

Nathan tugged on her hand again. "Come on, I helped make pancakes!"

Sienna laughed softly, knowing what a disaster her son could be in the kitchen. "You helped, huh?"

The scent of warm pancakes and fresh coffee wrapped around her as Nathan pulled her into the kitchen. She smiled, letting herself be tugged along, his small hand clutching hers. The buttery-sweet aroma filled the air, mingling with the faintest trace of spring flowers.

"Okay, you can open your eyes."

She opened them to see a plate of golden pancakes and syrup waiting on the chalk-painted table, the stack slightly uneven, as if put there by eager small hands. Her chest gave a little squeeze. Beside the table, Ethan stood drying his hands on a dish towel, a slight smirk tugging at his mouth as his gaze slid to her. He wore blue jeans and a cream sweater, the sleeves pushed up to his elbows, his hair still damp from a shower. His sweater and jeans were the same shade as hers, making them look— unintentionally—like a pair.

"Happy Mother's Day." His voice was low, his eyes softening when they met hers, and for a beat, the room went still in a way that had nothing to do with sound. The light from the window caught in his hair, turning the darker strands almost gold at the edges.

Sienna's heart stumbled on the moment, on the quiet steadiness of his presence. "Thank you." She offered a smile she hoped didn't betray the sudden nervous swirl in her tummy.

Ethan nodded to the table, already set with plates, cups, cutlery and a small vase of spring flowers she was pretty sure came from the narrow garden along the side of the house.

Releasing her hand, Nathan shot across the kitchen, arms spread wide. "We made you breakfast!" His words tumbled over themselves, excitement spilling out as he looked up at Ethan. "Daddy and me made you pancakes."

Her heart twisted so hard she almost had to reach for the counter to steady herself. *Daddy and me.* She should correct his grammar, but she didn't have the heart to spoil his excitement. Her throat tightened, and she pressed a hand briefly to her chest. The moment was so touching, she almost cried, but the last thing she wanted was to dampen this slice of simple joy Nathan had been waiting for his whole young life.

He darted to pull out a chair, his face alight with pride. "Happy Mother's Day, Mommy. Sit. Daddy said to pull out your chair for you."

"Thank you." She glanced at Ethan. He was already acing the role of father, giving their son lessons in chivalry. For a moment, the air between them stretched, something unspoken passing across the space. Then he glanced at Nathan, and she understood what the *something* was—*gratitude*. She only wished she hadn't waited so long to tell their son the truth. She wiped suddenly clammy hands on the thighs of her jeans, then eased onto the chair, tucking her hair behind her ear. She'd decided to wear it loose today in celebration of the special occasion.

Ethan reached past her to set a small glass of orange juice on the table, his arm brushing hers for the barest second. The contact sent an unexpected ripple of warmth through her. She glanced up, and for a heartbeat their eyes met. The look he gave her was unguarded, raw in a way she hadn't expected.

He straightened with a faint smile and rubbed the back of his neck. Nathan clambered up onto the chair beside her, kicking his feet with cheerful energy.

"We made extra special ones," her son announced proudly, pointing at the stack. "See? They're shaped like hearts."

Sienna's gaze dropped to the plate. She could easily distinguish the pancakes her son made from Ethan's. Some were uneven, lopsided and a little singed at the edges, but sure enough, they were molded into heart shapes. In the interest of fairness, she chose one slightly overdone, wonky heart-shaped pancake and one perfect one, then glanced at Ethan, who shrugged and returned her grin.

"Thank you, peanut." She reached over and stroked Nathan's cheek. "This is the best Mother's Day gift." The first one she'd ever had. Usually, Mother's Day passed without much recognition, apart from her calling her mom to wish her a special day. Nathan had been too young to make a fuss, so she never really celebrated. She'd forever treasure today as a special memory.

He grinned, puffing out his little chest. "Daddy helped."

"I can see that. Go, Daddy."

Nathan giggled, pumping his fist in the air. "Go, Daddy!"

With a chuckle, Ethan filled her cup with fresh-brewed coffee, then his, before placing the pot back on the counter. He pulled out the chair across from her and settled into it with a grace a man his size shouldn't have.

For the first time in a long while, Sienna let herself sit in the moment, let herself imagine, just for a second, what it might be like if this were their everyday.

Nathan tugged at her sleeve, voice bubbling. "Try one, Mommy. Daddy says they're really good."

She laughed softly, reaching for her fork and cutting into the pancake Nathan had made, the fluffy texture pulling apart easily. He leaned forward, his eyes bright as he eagerly awaited her verdict. She took a bite, tasting the buttery warmth and a hint of vanilla. It might have been slightly burnt, but it was, without a doubt, the best pancake she'd ever had.

She covered her mouth briefly, chuckling. "It's delicious."

Nathan let out a small whoop, fists punching the air.

Finally, after days of constant fear and danger, she could breathe. Just enjoy the moment.

She reached for the syrup. "Come on, guys, I can't eat all of these by myself."

Nathan giggled as Ethan delivered a small stack to Nathan's plate. Something warm flickered in the depth of his eyes as he watched his son. He then dished himself a stack of pancakes and gave her a smile, which she returned. She watched them quietly, her heart swelling and tightening at once. Nathan, wide-eyed and wriggly with excitement. Ethan, gentle and attentive, his large hand helping Nathan to squeeze the syrup bottle, steadying his son's hands with a patience that touched her as Nathan poured sticky lines across his pancakes.

This was what she'd longed for, secretly dreamed of for years. *Her family.* Not that they were truly a family in the sense of forever vows and promises, but Ethan would always own her heart. He was Nathan's father, and that made him her family. She'd agreed to move back to Hope Haven, which meant she needed to start looking for someplace for her and Nathan to live—if they made it that far. The thought sent a cold chill down her spine. She couldn't shake the knowledge that her deadly pursuers were still out there.

Still on the hunt.

Ethan reached for his coffee, then watched their son with a quiet fondness that softened the strong lines of his face. The warmth in his gaze caught her off guard. For a second, she saw not the man who'd once stood by her side, but the father their son needed. The man who, maybe one day, might forgive her.

She set her cup down. Where did they go from here?

The question hovered at the edge of her thoughts. She could see herself being back in Hope Haven, but what would she and Ethan even be? Co-parents? Friends? Two people too bruised to try again?

"More coffee?" The low, familiar rumble of Ethan's voice pulled her out of her thoughts. She glanced up, startled to find him standing beside her, coffeepot in hand.

"Sure." She held out her cup. The scent of coffee mingled with the clean scent of soap as he leaned in slightly to refill her cup. "Thank you."

He gave a short nod, his mouth curving faintly. "You're welcome."

"Thanks for this." She indicated the table with the remnants of breakfast. "You didn't have to."

He glanced at Nathan, who was weaving his fork through the air like a spaceship and smiled. "I'd say we have a few Mother's Days to make up for."

She buried her nose in her cup, inhaling the rich aroma of the coffee. "Not to mention Father's Days."

"And Father's Days." With a smile, Ethan reached up and brushed his thumb lightly along her hairline before bending and pressing a soft kiss to the top of her head. "Happy Mother's Day, Si."

Sienna closed her eyes, a faint tremble running through her. His gentleness, his closeness, the way his steady presence wrapped around her was a comfort she hadn't known she still yearned for, a reminder of all she had once longed for and now feared to hope for again.

He stepped back, just slightly. From the corner of her eye, she caught a glint outside the kitchen window.

Ethan placed the coffeepot on the table. "Sienna—"

The window over the sink exploded. Glass burst inward as the gunshot split the air, yanking Sienna's breath from her lungs.

Ethan was already moving. Grabbing her. Dragging her down.

Another shot rang out.

FIFTEEN

"Get down!" Ethan dove to the ground, taking Sienna with him. Her body slammed into his, her breath a sharp gasp against his collarbone.

Nathan screamed and dropped to the floor, wrapping his arms around his head.

"Nathan, don't move." She clambered off Ethan and reached for their son.

Another shot ripped through the cabinets, sending coffee grounds everywhere. Sienna clutched Nathan, muttering a desperate prayer.

Ethan lunged for the kitchen drawer beside the fridge, where he'd locked his Glock away.

"Get in the pantry." But Sienna was already ahead of him, crouching low with Nathan under her protective arm as she hurried with him to the safety of the pantry.

Ethan keyed in the code to the drawer, the sharp beep of the lock disengaging barely registering over the ringing in his ears. He yanked the drawer open, grabbed his Glock and dropped into a low crouch behind the island as another shot split the air.

Glass scattered across the counter and floor. Flour floated through the air like powdered snow and fell over spilled syrup and splintered ceramic. He edged toward the sink, crouched low, Glock steady in both hands. Glass crunched beneath his boots as he leaned into the corner of the window frame, careful not to silhouette himself.

Beyond the fractured remains of the window, he scanned the property. Roughly seventy yards out, near the border of the south field, a blue pickup sat just beyond the property line.

His jaw clenched. It looked like the one from the roadside ambush. Half concealed in the brush, angled for cover, but not enough to hide the metal glint of a rifle. The driver's door hung open. The truck had been parked on the rise of a shallow slope, giving the shooter a clean line of sight. A man stood in the bed of the truck, just behind the cab, his rifle braced across the roof, using it as a firing platform. Sunlight flickered off the scope as he adjusted his aim.

Ethan's stomach turned to stone.

He could see the man's form—broad-shouldered, gloved hands, dark clothing, a ball cap pulled low. Another shot took out the window, splintering the cupboard behind him. His phone vibrated in his jeans back pocket. He ignored it, drew a breath and steadied the Glock, keeping his aim on the gunman.

His phone started to vibrate again. This time he grabbed it, glancing to see Carter's name on his caller ID.

He hit the answer icon with his thumb and tossed the phone on the counter beside him. "Carter, I'm a little busy right now."

"I know it's Mother's Day, but I thought you'd like to know that Trip Anderson isn't dead. He's in the hospital in Idaho."

Ethan ripped his attention from the gunman and stared at his phone for a second. Had Sienna got it wrong, or had she deliberately kept that information from him? "Trip is alive?"

"Barely, but yes. He's sedated, and although it's been touch and go, his doctor tells me he expects him to make a full recovery."

A fresh round cracked through the air, yanking Ethan's focus back to the shooter.

"Is that gunfire?" Carter's voice jumped from conversational to high alert.

"Yeah, I've got a situation."

"I'm on my way."

"I've got this." But he was talking to dead air.

He locked on to the gunman's shoulder, keeping his breath even as he waited for the break in movement that would give him the shot.

The man adjusted his aim, preparing to shoot. Ethan aimed through the shattered window. He didn't shoot to kill. Not unless there was no other choice.

He squeezed the trigger.

The gunman jerked backward, his weapon flying out of his hands. He grabbed his arm, stumbled off the pickup bed and staggered out of sight, disappearing into the trees. Ethan held his position, waiting for the man to reappear. Every instinct urged him to pursue the gunman—to apprehend him, to get answers—but the stronger pull, the protective one, demanded he stay put.

The pickup matched the one that had ambushed them on the way to Elk Ridge too closely to ignore, and the guy hadn't been alone then. With the security system compromised, this could easily be a coordinated hit.

Pursuing the gunman meant leaving Sienna and Nathan exposed, and that was not an option. Not even for a minute. For all he knew, the others were out there—waiting, watching, hoping he'd take the bait and leave the house unguarded. Charging off into open terrain without backup wasn't bravery—it was recklessness. The smart move, the right move, was staying put and keeping the people who mattered most alive.

Carter was already on his way. Better to check on Sienna and Nathan, lock the place down and be ready for whatever came next. Because this might not be over. He straightened, tucked his gun in the back waistband of his jeans and crossed the kitchen, his boots crunching through the glass and broken ceramic. Coffee dripped from the edge of the table onto the floor and mixed with flour, cereal and ground coffee. The mess was total. But none of it mattered. He stepped past the wreckage and headed for the pantry.

"Sienna?" He eased the door open. "All clear. You're safe now."

She stepped out of the shadows, her arms tight around Nathan, his face tucked into the crook of her neck. He scanned them both quickly, relief pulsing through him when he didn't see blood or injuries. Nathan was pale and shaken, clinging to Sienna.

"Are you okay?" He met Sienna's gaze, but his hand brushed over his son's back. *Please, Lord, don't let this cause Nathan any long-term damage. Help him to overcome all that he has experienced these last few days.*

She nodded, surprisingly calm considering what just happened. "How did he get past your boundary security?"

Nathan turned toward Ethan, and Sienna handed him over without hesitation, like it was the most natural thing to do.

"Let's go see." He led the way to his office to check the monitor. It didn't take long to figure out the reason the gunman was able to get so close without alerting them. "I think they hacked it. Same as Carter's phone."

She turned wide eyes to him. "You said this was state of the art."

"Yeah. Which means we're up against someone with exceptional computer skills."

She dropped into the nearest chair, braced her elbows on her knees, leaned forward and sunk her fingers in her hair. "So, what's the next move?"

Sliding her fingers out of her hair, she stared at her hands, which were dusted in flour. Her hair and clothes were coated in it, and Nathan was the same. Ethan figured he hadn't escaped the flour bath either and probably looked worse.

"I'll call the company who installed the system and see if they can get it back online." The monitor flickered with static, reminding him of how vulnerable they were. He held Nathan close, rubbing his back in a slow, steady rhythm. "The gunman was driving a blue pickup that looks a lot like the one that ambushed us."

Sienna's gaze snapped to his. Even dusted head to toe in flour, she was still the most beautiful woman he'd ever seen. "It's the same men?"

"I'm pretty sure it is." He adjusted Nathan in his arms, holding him closer. "There was only one shooter. I caught him in the shoulder. He ran and left the pickup behind."

Her brows furrowed. "Do you think he'll return?"

"He's injured, so maybe not, but that doesn't mean his buddies won't try again."

Sienna buried her face in her hands. "Will this ever end?"

It could've been a rhetorical question, but he answered anyway. "I'll keep you and Nathan safe. Always." He reached out and stroked his hand over her hair. "Come here."

When she finally raised her face, her eyes were shimmering. She was working so hard to keep it together, it pinched his heart. He took her hand and urged her to her feet, then gave her a one-armed hug. She sagged against him, wrapping her arms around him and Nathan.

Nathan uncurled one arm from Ethan's neck and wrapped it around Sienna. "Don't cry, Mommy. Daddy will catch the bad men."

His son's confidence in him humbled him, making him vow silently never to let his son down, no matter what.

"Carter is coming over." He brushed a kiss to Sienna's hair. "When he gets here, he and I will secure the pickup. See if we can lift some prints."

She nodded, sniffled, then cleared her throat and stepped out of his embrace. "I'll go get us cleaned up."

"Good idea." He lowered Nathan to his feet. Ethan watched her closely, gauging her reaction to what he was about to tell her, searching to see whether this was news to her. "Carter called to tell me that Trip is in the hospital."

Sienna stilled, her breath catching. "Trip is alive?"

"Sedated. It's touch and go, but they're hopeful. The doctors think he'll survive."

She pressed a hand to her chest. "I thought he was…" She exhaled and met his eyes, shock plain in her expression. The tight band around Ethan's chest loosened. She wasn't faking it—she was genuinely rocked by the news. "That he was…the gun went off during his tussle with the big guy, and Trip fell to the floor. He wasn't moving. He looked like he was…" As though her legs didn't have the strength to hold her up any longer, she dropped back onto the chair. "Thank You, Lord." She swallowed, clearly trying to process the new update. Then her head jerked up, eyes locking with his. "We need to go see him. Maybe he can give us answers about who's behind all of this." She made a sweeping gesture with her hand.

He nodded. They both knew how badly they needed that kind of break.

Perched on the edge of the bed, Sienna held Ethan's phone to her ear, her thumb brushing the case absently as she watched Nathan play quietly across the room. The soft clatter of toys offered a fragile sense of normalcy, but her nerves were still on edge.

Ethan had instructed her not to use her phone until Dustin checked it, so she'd borrowed his to make the call. He'd called his parents to stay with her and Nathan while he and Carter swept the pickup for evidence.

After getting Nathan bathed, dressed in fresh clothes and

settled, she'd stood under the hot spray of the shower and tried to calm her racing mind. There were too many unknowns. Too many dangers still circling, and they were no closer to exposing the operation. If she couldn't find evidence to back up what her father had hinted at, she could lose everything she cherished.

The first step was to try to get ahold of the breeding records— proof that her father and Trip had sold falsely pedigreed horses as elite champions.

Jolene picked up on the fifth ring, her voice bright. "Blake Ranch Office. This is Jolene."

"Hi, Jolene, it's Sienna Blake. I hope I'm not catching you at a bad time."

"Oh! No, ma'am. Just paperwork and wranglin' invoices."

"On a Sunday?"

"It's a busy ranch." She gave a light tinkling laugh. "What can I do for you?"

Sienna kept her tone even. "The other day while sorting through my dad's papers, I realized I couldn't find the horse records—stallion logs, breeding charts, that sort of thing. I was wondering if you've seen them in the office."

Jolene gave the tinkling laugh again. "Well, I sure wish I could be more help, but I didn't start here till after your daddy passed. Mason hired me on not long after he took over. I mostly deal with new contracts and ranch scheduling. Don't know much about the old stuff."

"You haven't seen any older files tucked away?"

"Not that I recall, but I'll gladly poke around. Sometimes things get shuffled when we move boxes. I'll take a peek in the storage drawer and see if any files are where they don't belong."

"I'd appreciate that. Thank you."

"Course. Happy to help. How are y'all doin', by the way? After that loft scare? Lord have mercy, when I heard that crash, I just about jumped outta my skin. We came runnin' soon as we heard it."

"Thank you for your help that day." The memory of creaking beams and splintering wood flashed through her mind, sending a jolt of remembered fear through her. "We're all right."

"Thank the Lord. It could've been a whole lot worse. I mean, I had no idea that old barn was ready to collapse. It looked sturdy enough. I woulda never guessed it'd give way just like that."

"I don't think it gave out on its own."

"It didn't?"

"Ethan doesn't think it was an accident."

"My word. Are you serious?" Jolene's surprise pitched her voice higher. "Now who in the world would do a thing like that?"

"We're still trying to figure it out." Every answer unearthed more questions. She focused on Nathan, who was busy making Woody arrest a bad guy. He'd already been through more than any five-year-old should. But in his world, the good guys still won. And she'd do whatever it took to keep it that way. She drew in a breath and slowly released it. He trusted Woody to bring justice. She had to trust God to do the same.

"Well, that's just awful. I'll keep an eye out, Sienna. And if those files you're looking for turn up, you'll be the first to know."

"Thanks, Jolene."

"Anytime. You take care, now." Jolene's peppy response did little to convince Sienna she'd ever see those records.

She echoed Jolene's sentiment and ended the call. The silence that followed felt heavier somehow.

They had to find those files. Without them, she had zero evidence—no way to prove what Trip and her father were caught up in or who else might be involved. Trip was alive. The news had stunned her. But now, there was hope. He had answers. He could tell her who her father had feared and who the boss really was.

They needed to go see him in the hospital as soon as possible.

Her pulse picked up. The gunman had mentioned his boss, and her dad had told her this was bigger than all of them. But it was the genuine fear in her dad's eyes that had convinced her the boss was someone utterly ruthless. Someone willing to eliminate her and anyone who got in his way. Someone powerful and callous enough to hire men to do his dirty work.

My boss doesn't do extensions.

The gunman's statement echoed in her mind, chilling her to her core.

SIXTEEN

Ethan stepped through the hospital's automatic doors with Sienna. The sharp scent of antiseptic, edged with that familiar sterile chill, hit him immediately. One breath of it, and he was back on a gurney with blood soaking through his shirt, pain firing like lightning through his body.

Six years, and the memory was still sharp. The bullet had struck just above the ridge of his left shoulder blade, fracturing the bone and knocking him to the ground before he even heard the shot. For days, the medical team hadn't been sure he'd make it. The doctors had called it a lucky break. Said that an inch lower and he wouldn't have survived.

But Ethan knew it hadn't been luck. It was only by God's grace that the bullet had landed where it did. He could acknowledge that now. His shoulder ached at the memory, a dull, familiar pull that hadn't fully gone away. Some days it stiffened enough to remind him he wasn't invincible.

He'd once felt that way with Sienna by his side. Like nothing could touch them. Then he'd woken up after surgery to find that she'd left him—disappeared without a goodbye.

Ethan glanced at her walking beside him in the hospital corridor. He'd carried anger for so long, he hadn't thought he'd ever be able to forgive her. But here she was, and for the first time since she walked back into his life, he wasn't sitting in the wreckage of the past. He was looking to the future. Uncertainty stretched ahead of them, but one thing was clear, he couldn't bear to lose the fragile reconnection they'd found.

He pressed the call button for the elevator. The doors swished open immediately and they stepped inside.

Sienna hugged her arms around her middle, worry flickering in her eyes. As the elevator doors slid shut, she met his gaze. "When the man threatened Trip, he mentioned his boss. Do you think Trip will give us his name?"

Tension tightened her face, and her eyes were shadowed from too little sleep. She looked on edge, and he understood why. Trip was their only real lead—the one person who had the information they desperately needed. If they had any hope of putting a name to the threat stalking Sienna and Nathan, this was it.

He rolled his shoulders to release the sudden tension. "If he knows, I'll make sure he tells us."

She shifted her weight, eyes searching his face. "Wouldn't that put him in danger?"

He met her concerned gaze. "If it does, he won't be left exposed. We've got procedures for that."

They'd already seen the ruthless way these people went about covering their tracks—the way they'd callously disrupted Mother's Day, turning it into a memory none of them would forget for all the wrong reasons.

By the time Carter arrived and they reached the edge of the property, the pickup had already gone. All that remained was shell casings, tire marks and churned earth. Either the shooter had doubled back or his buddies had returned for the truck. With little else to go on, he and Carter had collected what evidence they could. He'd spoken to Grant, who'd had a solid alibi for the time the semi had been on the road. He'd been visiting his mother in Sacramento for two days, which put him too far away to have been involved.

Dustin had checked Sienna's phone and hadn't found any spyware, hidden apps or unauthorized access logs. Her phone was clean. But, as Ethan had suspected, the semi had been hacked and remotely controlled. Dustin hadn't been able to trace the user; they'd wiped all the data that could lead back to them.

The elevator doors opened, and Ethan and Sienna stepped into the quiet ICU lobby. Muted lighting softened the sterile white walls, and the faint beep of monitors filtered through double doors down the hall. A middle-aged nurse in burgundy scrubs behind the station looked up from her clipboard as they approached.

Ethan flashed his badge. "Sheriff Ethan Callahan, Hope Haven Sheriff's Department. We're here to see a patient—Trip Anderson."

"Oh." The nurse's expression shifted. "I'm sorry, Sheriff. Mr. Anderson passed away early this morning."

Beside him, Sienna's breath caught.

He slipped his badge into his pocket. "What happened?"

"He went into cardiac arrest." She hugged the clipboard to her chest. "He'd been stable through the night, but around five thirty, his heart stopped. The team did everything they could, but he never regained consciousness."

He met Sienna's gaze. He could see she was thinking the same thing he was. Trip had survived the initial injury, clung to life for days and now—just when they were close to answers—he was gone.

Sienna's gaze flicked back to the nurse. "We were told he was expected to make a full recovery."

She gave a little shrug. "Like I said, he suddenly went into cardiac arrest."

Something about this didn't sit right with Ethan. "Was there anyone with him when it happened?"

The nurse hesitated, then frowned slightly. "A doctor was in with him. That's why we were able to start resuscitation immediately. But there was nothing anyone could do. His heart just wouldn't restart."

He'd seen the lengths these people were willing to go. Would they go this far? "Who was the doctor with him?"

"Oh…" The nurse frowned as she thought for a moment. "I don't know. I hadn't seen him before."

A sinking sensation weighed down Ethan's stomach. "Can you describe him?"

"He was quite tall—kinda big—and was wearing a lab coat, same as all the other doctors, but he had on a ball cap. We don't have any doctors on duty who wear hats—especially not in the ICU. I figured he must've been new." She shrugged. "Part of the critical care team."

Ethan's pulse ticked higher, but he kept his voice even. "Do you have cameras on this floor?"

"Yes, in the hallway, stairwell and elevator lobby."

"Have security pull the footage from this morning. I want to see everyone who entered or exited Trip Anderson's room." If they caught the man on camera, there was a good chance they might have captured his face.

The nurse nodded. "I'll alert security." She reached for the desk phone, then looked up at him. "Do you want someone to meet you in the lobby?"

"That'd be best. I want to review the footage before we leave."

Sienna shifted beside him. She didn't have to say a word. He read her thoughts in the look she gave him. If someone had slipped past the hospital's safeguards in plain sight, impersonating a doctor to eliminate a witness, it confirmed a chilling level of confidence and calculated intent. And proved there wasn't anything they wouldn't do.

The nurse tapped the phone with a fingernail, waiting for the line to connect. "I'll let them know you're on your way."

"Thanks." Ethan turned with Sienna and headed to the elevators. "Did the man she described sound like the one you saw Trip arguing with?"

Sienna puffed out a breath. "She was pretty vague, but big, tall and wearing a ball cap sounds familiar."

"Yeah, I thought so, too."

Sienna's phone dinged and she retrieved it from her jeans pocket as they walked. With a sudden stillness that sent a ripple of unease through him, she stopped mid-step, staring at the screen.

As she stared at her phone, her pulse hitched. The text came from a number she didn't recognize.

I have the proof you're looking for. Meet me tonight at 8. North barn at Blake Ranch. Come alone.

"What is it?" Concern edged Ethan's deep voice. "Is Nathan okay?"

She nodded. If something had gone wrong, his parents would have contacted him. "He's fine." Grace and James had leaped at the chance to babysit their grandson. Nathan, in turn, had been excited to spend the day with his grandparents, which hadn't surprised her since they enjoyed spoiling him as much as he enjoyed being spoiled. Apart from herself and Ethan, they were the only people she trusted with her son.

"The text isn't from your parents. I think it's from Jolene." She turned the screen for Ethan to see. "I asked her to have a look for the missing files. Maybe she found them."

Ethan cocked one eyebrow. "How do you know the text is from Jolene? That number isn't in your contacts."

"It's the logical conclusion. She's the only one I spoke to about the files. We didn't exchange cell numbers, which is why it comes up as unfamiliar."

He stabbed the call button for the elevator. "If you didn't exchange numbers, how did she get yours?"

"Uncle Mason, maybe?" The elevator doors opened, and she

entered the confined space alongside Ethan, who looked skeptical. "I don't know. The point is, someone is willing to give us the proof we've been searching for. Sadly, Trip isn't here to tell us who the boss is. If these really are the breeding records I saw all those years ago, they might lead us to the man behind all of this. And we'd have proof of the bloodline fraud."

"This could be a trap."

The doors closed, and the elevator began its slow descent.

"What if it really is Jolene? What if she found something and doesn't know who to trust?"

Ethan exhaled and raked a hand through his hair, leaving it tousled. Something about the unconscious gesture tugged at her heart. "And what if it's not Jolene?"

She expelled her breath. He had a point, but could she really ignore this message? They needed this breakthrough. "Then it'd be confirmation that someone's trying to draw me out."

"That's not a comfort."

"No." She dropped her gaze to the phone. The message stared back at her from the glowing screen. Either way she needed to find out. "But I'm going."

"Not on your own."

"It says to come alone." She slipped the phone into her pocket.

Ethan folded his arms across his wide chest. "Doesn't matter what the text says, Sienna. Your safety's too important not to take proper precautions."

Her safety was too important.

Was he speaking as the sheriff or as the man who once asked her to marry him? Did he mean she was important to him, or was he just protecting a witness?

She pushed her fingers into the front pockets of her jeans. "Okay, what are the precautions?"

When he glanced her way, the gentleness in his expression caught her off guard, making her pulse skip.

His jaw flexed, telling her he didn't like agreeing to this. "I'll be close, Carter will be on standby and Dustin can monitor from the perimeter."

Her heart thudded. "So, I go in?"

"You go in *only* if we control the conditions." He glanced at her, the steel in his voice tempered by something gentler. "I won't take chances with you."

She swallowed hard, nodding once. There was no arguing with that tone—not from the sheriff and not from the man who'd once held her heart.

SEVENTEEN

A glance over her shoulder drew Sienna's gaze to the rise of the east pasture, where a narrow gravel track climbed toward a dense stand of firs. At the top of the incline, tucked in shadow, the surveillance van waited—barely visible in the fading light. Ethan was lying low, positioned close enough to reach her within seconds if she needed him. Carter and Dustin were inside listening, tracking her location, ready to move the second anything went wrong.

She couldn't see Ethan, but that didn't matter. He was close. Watching. Waiting. And that gave her courage.

Her fingers brushed the discreet device tucked inside her ear, hidden by her hair. Ethan had insisted she wear the secure comm, had walked her through every step before she left the van. *Don't enter until I give the all-clear, keep your back to a wall if possible, trust your instincts. Get out of there if anything seems hinky.* She'd followed his instructions without argument. His presence offered a comfort she hadn't realized she needed.

But now, with Ethan's go-ahead, she stood at the threshold of the yawning barn doors. Behind her, the sky was darkening to indigo, deepening the shadows, steeping the barn in eerie silence. Her pulse flickered at the base of her throat as she scanned the interior.

"No one's here." She kept her voice barely above a whisper.

The device in her ear crackled softly. "You're sure the barn's empty?"

She scanned the interior. Shafts of moonlight slipped through cracked slats in the walls and the windows above, casting thin silver stripes across the dusty floor. A few overturned barrels. Piles of scattered hay. The splintered mess of the collapsed loft still covered part of the space near the back, along with boxes and strewn papers. The wreckage was still cordoned off with caution tape.

"Yeah, I'm sure. There's no one here." On edge, she finger-combed her hair back from her face. "Maybe I'm early."

"You're on time."

"I'll go inside, see if they left the file." A solitary hoot echoed across the pasture, the mournful cry raising goose bumps on her arms.

"Stay vigilant." Ethan's voice crackled softly through her comm, close despite the distance.

"I will." She stepped in farther, the crunch of grit under her boots too loud in the stillness.

"What do you see?"

"It's pretty much the way we left it." Her voice dropped as she moved toward the debris. "The tape is still up. The boxes and loft timber are still lying on the ground."

"If the person behind the message doesn't show up in the next couple minutes, get out of there."

"Jolene might just be running late." She kept her back to the wall, eyes scanning the barn's shadowed interior, making sure no one was lurking in the shadows.

"You don't know it's her." Ethan lowered his voice to a firm cadence. "Don't let your guard down, Si." The way he said her name always had a way of calming her.

"Okay." Her phone buzzed in her back pocket. The vibration jolted her. She yanked it free. Pulse quickening, she swiped open the message.

I told you to come alone.

Her stomach dropped. "I just got a text." Her breath locked in her throat. "It's from the unknown number."

"What does it say?"

"'I told you to come alone.'" Her voice trembled. She drew in a deep breath and steadied it. "Maybe she's scared."

Ethan's rough breath filtered into her ear. "Si, don't assume anything. And especially not that you're dealing with Jolene. This could be anyone."

"I'm texting back." She began typing, her thumbs flying over the keys as she murmured the words under her breath.

You can trust me. If you're worried, leave the file somewhere and I'll pick it up.

She hit Send and waited, breath locked in her throat.
Three dots appeared. Then disappeared.
Then came the reply.

No. It has to be in person. I'll contact you again soon.

Sienna stared at the message, a sick twist of disappointment churning in her stomach. So close. They'd been so close. She pressed the phone to her chest, willing her frustration down as she read the text to Ethan.

He blew out a breath. "Doesn't look like they're going to show. Let's call it."

She closed her eyes, let the disappointment settle.

"Come on out, Sienna."

"I'm on my way."

She turned toward the exit, boots crunching over the debris-strewn floor, her phone still gripped tight in one hand. This was the second time in days they'd come close to a breakthrough only to have it slip away. Every time she thought they were making progress, the path twisted just out of reach.

She stepped out into the cooler night air and caught sight of a figure standing in the shadows. Tall. Broad-shouldered. Familiar.

Her breath escaped in a surprised rush, and the fine hairs on her body stood on end.

"Uncle Mason?" Relief sliced through her. It was only her uncle—not the man hunting her. He was still out there somewhere, and they had no idea who he was. The hospital security footage hadn't given them a break. The cameras had captured him entering Trip's room dressed like any other doctor, except he was wearing a baseball cap, then minutes later, nurses rushing in behind him. The cameras also recorded him leaving but never caught his face. He'd kept his head down, the peak of his ball cap angled perfectly to shield his features from every angle.

With a warm smile, Mason stepped forward, hands spread in a gesture of welcome. "Well, look what the wind blew in."

She smiled, the tension in her shoulders easing just a little. "Hey."

Mason crossed the remaining distance and pulled her into a brief fatherly hug. His familiar scent—soap and leather—brought a tangle of emotions she wasn't prepared for. He hadn't changed much. A few more lines around his eyes, maybe, his hair and mustache whiter, but he was the same steady presence she remembered from childhood.

When he pulled back, his gaze scanned her face. "Didn't expect to find you poking around out here this time of night, kid. Everything all right?"

"I, uh…" She glanced toward the barn. "I wanted to take another look at Dad's papers. The boxes were still out here after the loft collapsed."

Mason patted her arm. "I don't know what happened to cause the collapse, but we're helping the Sheriff's department find out." He hugged her again, hard enough to squeeze the breath from her lungs. "I'm glad you're okay."

Sienna chuckled, easing out of the bear hug. Uncle Mason always did give big burly hugs.

"Thanks." She glanced back to the barn. "I hope you don't mind."

"Mind?" He gave a rumbling chuckle. "Darlin', this will always be your home. You don't have to ask permission."

That caught her off guard. How easily those words turned her heart over. She swallowed and nodded, the truth catching behind her ribs. Should she tell him why she was really there?

"Don't do it." Ethan's voice in her ear sent a jolt through her. How did he know what she was thinking?

She couldn't respond, since she would look like a crazy person talking to herself in the middle of their conversation.

"I haven't seen you in years." Mason's craggy voice gentled. "I'm sorry I wasn't here when you came by last week." He dropped his arm around her shoulders, pulling her into his side. "Stay a while. Let's visit. I'd like to catch up." He gestured toward the dirt path that ran alongside the barn. "Walk with me? The night air does a man good after a long day."

Sienna hesitated. Her instinct was to get back to Ethan, to safety. But Mason wasn't a stranger. He was family. And if she was honest, she *did* want to talk to him—especially after what they'd discovered. Maybe she could ask him the questions that had been clawing at her. Like how did her dad manage to overdose?

"Are you sure that's a good idea?" Ethan's voice came over the comm.

"Yes, that's a good idea." She fell into step beside Mason. "It'd be nice to catch up, but I'll need a lift home later." She hoped Ethan got the message. She was safe with Mason, and they could leave.

"Si, I don't like the idea of leaving you out here without backup."

Mason tightened his hug around her shoulders, squeezing her to him. "I'll drive you myself."

"Perfect. I know I'm in good hands." Ethan was smart, he'd get the message.

"I get it." He blew out a breath and she pictured him raking his hand through his hair, the way he did when he was holding back frustration. "You're safe and I can stand down. I still don't like it. Keep the comm on."

Mason smiled at her. "It's good to see you, kid."

"And you, Uncle Mason." She touched his hand on her shoulder. "I've been looking forward to catching up."

"There's so much I have to tell you."

In her ear, she heard Ethan giving the order for Carter and Dustin to stand down. Heard the van doors open and Ethan's conversation with them. He wasn't happy about the turn of events, but there wasn't much she could do about that. Mason was her uncle, and he might have the answers she needed. But how would she know if she didn't ask him?

The conversation in the van was distracting her, so she discreetly removed the earpiece and slipped it into her pocket.

They walked in comfortable silence for a few paces, the steady rhythm of their footsteps crunching softly over gravel. The wind had picked up, rustling through the trees and stirring the scent of fresh-cut lumber and damp earth.

She adjusted her stride to match his, the chill of the wind slipping beneath her jacket. "Where are we going?"

"I want to show you our new rehab block." His arm was heavy on her shoulder, offering her warmth.

"You're building a rehab wing?" She glanced up at her uncle, awed and deeply touched.

He nodded, his expression somber. "Your dad used to talk about it all the time, remember?"

"Yes, I remember."

"In honor of Jacob, I've added the rehab block. Hydrotherapy, recovery stalls, even a padded treadmill lane once it's all installed."

Ahead, the new stable block loomed dark and quiet, its outer walls wrapped in scaffolding and fresh timber. Sienna stepped inside. The scent of clean timber and lime-washed stone filled the air—faint traces of varnish, industrial disinfectant and something faintly floral beneath. Not a single stall was occupied yet, but the design made her pause.

Mason flicked a switch, and the whole place lit up. He gestured to the open space with quiet pride. "What do you think?"

Her breath caught. "It's amazing." She stepped farther into the space, turning in a slow circle, the clean lines and newness of it all drawing her in. Thoughtful design was everywhere— from the stall spacing to the airflow. Every detail was purposeful, designed for comfort, safety and function. She gave a sad smile. "Dad would have loved this."

"Figured it was time." Mason's smile crinkled his eyes. "Horses work hard around here. They deserve better aftercare. Besides, the ranch needs to move with the times. And you..."

He glanced her way, the invitation unspoken but clear.

She swallowed hard. A space like this was a dream for any equine physiotherapist. A purpose-built facility. Modern equipment. The kind of system she'd only seen in elite equine rehab centers.

"I thought maybe you'd want to head this up." He patted the polished wood. "Assuming you're planning to stay."

Her heart gave a slow, uncertain flutter. She ran a hand along the smooth edge of the nearest stall divider, letting her fingertips trace the wood grain. She could see herself here. Working. Healing. Building something meaningful again.

And yet...

Ethan drifted into her thoughts. When he'd looked at her on

Mother's Day, she'd almost believed they hadn't completely lost what they once had. That maybe he'd forgiven her. But then the bullets started flying and the moment was lost—it seemed, forever—because Ethan hadn't come close to looking at her like that again. Yet, she couldn't help hoping they still had a future.

"I'll be staying." If only for Nathan's sake. She turned her face slightly away from Mason and focused on the layout in front of her, trying to ground herself in the present. "This is…" She cleared her throat, which had gone suddenly thick. Not from thinking about what she might, or might not, have with Ethan, she told herself. It was because her uncle had done a good thing in honor of her dad. "It's incredible. The horses are going to thrive here."

"I hoped you'd think so." His smile was gentle, proud. "Come on. There's something else I want you to see. A feature I added with you in mind."

She followed him without hesitation, weaving through the rows of empty stalls. The silence in the block was peaceful. As if the place was waiting to be filled with life.

He slowed near the back, beside a wide enclosed bay. "Designed this one as a recovery suite. For trauma cases. Heated flooring, vet access on both sides, lighting dimmable for rest cycles. You'd know how to use it better than anyone."

Moving back to Hope Haven meant starting over. She'd need a place for her and Nathan to live—and a job. And here was Uncle Mason offering her the perfect one. It was one less problem to navigate. Returning with a position already in place would simplify the transition. If she didn't have to job-hunt, she could focus entirely on finding the right home to raise her son.

"I'd be honored." She moved farther inside, taking it all in—the rubberized flooring, the larger-than-average stall bays, climate-control systems discreetly mounted above the windows. But what stilled her wasn't the stalls. It was the long glass-fronted enclosure built into the far wall, its interior lined with waterproof panels and stainless-steel fittings. A submerged treadmill bay.

Her eyes widened. "This is a top-of-the-line hydro unit."

Mason's smile deepened. "Still needs the filtration system, but yeah. Full aqua treadmill. We'll be able to do cold saltwater and warm whirlpool sessions."

Her fingertips brushed the control panel mounted beside the bay. "This alone changes everything."

"Does it?" The words themselves didn't alert her; it was Mason's tone that had her gaze jerking to him. His disarming smile confused her. His quiet, measured tone had stiffened her spine. But looking at him now, he was the same old Uncle Mason. "I'm glad you're on board." That same warm smile curved his mouth, the one she'd known since childhood. But it didn't reach his eyes. "It'll be good to have you here. There's just one issue we need to iron out."

She straightened, something cold creeping into her gut. "What's that?"

He stepped into the aisle, casually blocking the way to the exit. "Forget what you saw."

Her pulse hitched. A chill ran down her spine. He couldn't be saying what she thought he was. "What do you mean?"

"The bloodline records." The smoothness in his tone didn't match the steel in his eyes. "And what you overheard at Trip's ranch."

The air grew thin, making her breath shallow. "How do you know about that?"

"I know everything, Sienna. That's why I own this state."

He *was* the richest man in Montana. And right now, that felt far more dangerous than impressive.

A slow, dawning realization hit her.

"*You* were behind the threat that made me leave." She took a backward step, anxious to put space between them. "And behind the attempt on Ethan's life." The last couple of weeks flashed through her mind like a montage of horrifying moments. The semi bearing down on them. The man in her room. Nathan crying uncontrollably. Ethan's patrol truck exploding. The roadside ambush. The barn loft collapsing. The shooter on Mother's Day.

All of it was Mason?

She covered her face, heart pounding, disbelief and betrayal rushing in all at once. Everything in her resisted believing her beloved uncle could be someone so far from the person she thought she knew and loved.

"You should've stayed gone." He folded his arms, voice flat. "But instead, you came back. Started digging. And now, like your father, you've become a problem."

She could barely find her voice. "You—you're responsible for Dad's overdose? Why? He—he looked up to you. He *trusted* you."

"And that was his mistake." Mason didn't flinch. "Jacob was in deep. He knew the deal. But after you left town—"

"I was forced out of town. I didn't want to leave Ethan." Nausea rolled her stomach. All this time, and the villain was her own family. "Why did you kill Dad? To take his ranch?"

"He started getting…sentimental. Guilt made him sloppy." Her stomach turned.

"Wanted to come clean. Expose the operation," Mason continued. "Started wishing he'd handled things differently with you." He paused. "Weakness like that can't exist in my world."

"So you killed him?" she whispered. "Because he loved me?"

Mason met her gaze without a hint of remorse. "Because he got soft, kid. Sentimentality is bad for business. It gets people killed."

She hadn't even realized she was crying until a sob caught her off guard.

"Oh, honey, don't go messin' up that pretty face with tears."

Sienna's head shot up, her gaze searching for the woman whose voice came from behind Mason. Sienna spotted Jolene sauntering into the rehab block beside the big guy from Trip's ranch. The same man who'd been showing up ever since. He might've successfully hidden his face from the hospital security cameras, but the way he moved told Sienna he was the man who'd impersonated a doctor and was possibly responsible for Trip's death.

"Jolene?" She glanced at Mason, who didn't seem surprised that Jolene was with the man who had been hunting her. "Uncle Mason? What's going on?" What a stupid question. Sienna knew what was going on, but her brain rejected the obvious explanation, in the hope that Mason wasn't the callous man she was discovering him to be. "You're the boss?"

Like any good villain worth his salt, he left her to draw her own conclusions. Her brain was working overtime to piece it all together.

She stared at Jolene. "You texted me?"

"You should've come alone, Sienna." Jolene raised her hand, letting Sienna see the file she was holding. She flipped it open to reveal it was empty. "This could have been so painless."

"Painless?" Her brain zipped through a dozen connotations. She swung her gaze back to Mason. "Are you going to kill me, too?"

Mason laughed.

Jolene laughed.

The big guy laughed.

Sienna backed up a couple more steps, sank trembling fingers into her jeans front pocket. Her fingers closed on the comm, and she snatched it out.

"Ethan, help!" she yelled into the device before shoving it into her ear. Why had she removed it? And why had she sent Ethan away? She should've listened to him. He never trusted Mason, but her love for the uncle she thought he was blinded her. "Ethan?"

All she heard was static.

"Sorry, honey. I had to block your signals." Jolene held up a compact electronic device with a blinking red light and a short antenna. It looked harmless—like a glorified key fob— but when she pressed a button, the static in Sienna's earpiece became a deafening squeal, making her pluck it from her ear. She reached for her phone.

Jolene offered her a syrupy-sweet smile, all fake pity and no remorse. "Looks like your phone isn't working, either."

It didn't take a genius to figure out that sweet Southern belle Jolene was Mason's tech mastermind—the one behind the semi hacking, Carter's compromised phone, and the breach that disabled Ethan's new security system.

Sienna's nerves jangled.

"I don't want to hurt you, Sienna…but I will." Mason gave the big guy a slight nod, and he closed in on Sienna. "All you need to do is forget everything you know about the bloodline records and join us. You could run all this." Mason spread his arms wide. "Just think how much good you could do with a state-of-the-art rehabilitation center like this?"

Please, Lord, help me.

"The problem with that is I've got a strong sense of right and wrong, and no amount of bribery is going to stop me from bringing you to justice." She stepped back. "So I'll have to pass on your offer."

"I'm sorry to hear that, kid. I really am." One glance from Mason and the big guy lunged.

Sienna pivoted on her heels and ran, Mason's words echoed in her mind—*Vet access on both sides.*

There was another way out.

She sprinted left, aiming for the corner of the recovery suite, where she'd seen the access door. Her heart slammed against her ribs as she reached it, shoved it open and burst through.

After years of living here, Sienna didn't hesitate. She knew exactly where to run. Heavy footfalls pounded behind her, but she didn't look back. She tore across the path behind the rehab block, heading straight for the old abandoned stables beyond.

The distance to safety looked like miles, but she finally crashed through the heavy doors and bolted them before Mason's goon reached her. Her lungs burned. A stitch stabbed her side. But she was alive. Now she just had to find a way to contact Ethan.

She slipped the comm back into her ear. Nothing but static.

A quick check of her phone confirmed what she already knew—it was dead.

Sienna had no way of letting Ethan know she needed him. And it was her own fault. She scanned the dark interior, searching for something—anything—she could use as a weapon.

Then two things dawned on her at once.

The big guy wasn't trying to break the door down. And an ominous hiss was coming from the far end of the stables. She took a cautious step in that direction, heart thudding.

An explosion tore through the stable block, shaking the ground and hurling her off her feet. Heat and smoke slammed into her as the world flipped sideways.

Then everything went black.

EIGHTEEN

The blast rocked the night.

Ethan jerked upright, heart slamming as the concussive boom split the silence. A plume of firelit smoke spiraled into the sky, galvanizing him into action. He sprinted in the direction of the blast, jamming the comm in his ear. The high-pitched squeal from earlier still rang in his eardrum, but if there was even a chance the comm worked now, he had to try.

Thank God he hadn't stood down and left as she'd wanted him to. There'd been something gnawing at his gut, an uneasy feeling compelling him to stay put. He didn't have a reason to suspect things might go wrong, only a deep need to stay close until Sienna had finished visiting with her uncle. Now, that same unease became a thousand times more intense. And the feeling that she needed his help was stronger than instinct—it was a prompting too urgent to ignore.

"Sienna!" Years of navigating intense situations kept his voice steady, even as his pulse skyrocketed. "Sienna, do you read?"

Static hissed back. Someone had jammed their signal. He removed the comm, tossing it as his boots pounded the gravel. In seconds he caught sight of the blaze licking the roof of the stable block. Needles of icy dread pierced him.

He couldn't lose her.

Not again.

The flames were crawling fast across the roofline. If Sienna was in there, she wouldn't have long. Not at the rate the fire was engulfing the block. He sprinted toward the front of the stables and the double doors, the acrid bite of smoke clogging his throat. The wide doors were wedged shut with a metal rod threaded through the handles.

His heart slammed harder, fear clawing at his chest. Someone had done this on purpose—made sure she couldn't get out. If he had any questions about whether or not Sienna was on the other side of these doors, all doubt was gone now. There would be no other reason for the doors to be sealed shut like this.

Lord, I love her. Help me to save her. Please, don't take her from me. If You give me another chance, I promise not to waste it. I forgive her. I forgive her for everything. Please, Lord, don't let me be too late.

In one swift motion, he seized the rod and yanked it free, tossed it aside with a clatter and wrenched open the doors almost in one motion.

Smoke burst out in a suffocating wave, and so did Sienna. He released the doors, lunged forward, and caught her before she hit the ground. She tumbled into his arms, her body limp, breath rattling as she collapsed against his chest. She must have been leaning against the door.

"The Lord is my strength…and my shield…" Her voice was a thready, hoarse whisper as she weakly recited Psalm 28:7.

"I've got you." Ethan gathered her close. "I've got you, sweetheart. You're safe." Her head lolled against his shoulder. She coughed once, then stilled.

"Sienna?" He scooped her up, forcing back the surge of panic threating to paralyze him.

"Hmmm…" Her breath stuttered as she sagged against him.

"Stay with me, Si." Cradled protectively in his arms, he carried her away from the blaze as the flames roared louder behind them. The fire had claimed the building, but it hadn't taken her.

Thank You, Lord. Thank You.

He held her tighter. He'd almost lost her—this time for good. And in that split second, every wall he'd ever built between them crumbled. All the anger he'd carried—all the hurt—suddenly felt insignificant. He'd lived in fear that she'd leave him again. But today proved it could happen even when she had no control over it.

At a safe distance, he dropped to his knees, lowering her to the grass. "Si, talk to me."

She drew in broken breaths as she clutched his shirt, her voice raspy, raw from smoke. "It's Mason…" Her eyes fluttered, but her focus locked on his. "He's—he's the boss…killed Dad…" She gasped for breath. "Don't…let him…get away… Jolene…bad, too."

The surveillance van peeled into the yard, snagging Ethan's attention. Carter and Dustin jumped out.

"Call fire and ambulance." Ethan cradled Sienna against his chest as she curled into another bout of coughing. He tightened his hold, steadying her.

"Already done." Carter rushed over while Dustin retrieved the med kit from the van.

"It's Mason. He's the one behind it all—the boss." Ethan gently eased Sienna onto the grass. "Stay with her. I have to find him before he gets away."

As if on cue, a horse whinnied, and hoofs galloped out of the westside stables. Mason appeared, mounted and riding hard, his silhouette cutting through the shadows as he veered toward the back pasture. Everything in Ethan wanted to give chase, but he had to make sure Sienna was safe.

Seconds after, one of the ranch trucks gunned to life. Headlights flared, tires spitting dust as the truck sped past, Jolene at the wheel. She tore out onto the gravel road, speeding into the dark.

"Don't let her get away." Ethan threw the order at Carter,

who ran and jumped in behind the wheel of the surveillance van, giving chase.

He glanced at Dustin. "Stay with Sienna." Ethan eased her into a comfortable position, worry clouding his mind when she gave a soft groan, followed by another coughing fit and labored breathing. "Don't let anything happen to her."

"I won't." Shoving his glasses up his nose, Dustin dropped to his knees with the portable oxygen tank in hand.

"I'm going after him." Torn between staying to care for the woman he loved and apprehending a criminal, Ethan's pulse kicked up. He sprinted for the side paddock, vaulting over the rail when he caught sight of a ranch hand approaching from the trail at a canter, probably returning from checking water lines or moving stock for the night.

Ethan reached for his badge. "Sheriff Callahan." He flashed it. "I need your horse."

The young man reined in the gelding, swung down without hesitation. "Yes, sir."

Ethan was already grabbing the reins. "Appreciate it." He mounted in a smooth swing, wheeled the gelding around and kicked into a gallop, heading straight for the ridgeline.

Moonlight shimmered across the ridge, guiding his path. He'd seen which way Mason had gone, and Ethan had every intention of cutting him off before he reached the helipad.

Cool oxygen blasted into her lungs, sharp and jarring after the thick, acrid smoke. At first, her body rejected it—still racked by coughs, her ribs seizing with each breath. It burned going in, stung all the way down. Like breathing through a cracked window in winter. Her throat scraped raw, chest tight, eyes watering, but the air kept coming. Each inhale dragged cool, clean air into her starved lungs.

Slowly, relief crept in. But the panic hadn't vanished. It lingered in her limbs, in the memory of not being able to breathe, in the smoky echo still clinging to the back of her throat. But each breath stretched a little deeper. A little steadier.

She was alive. *Thank You, Father!*

Every fiber in her body whispered gratitude.

Her eyes drifted shut. Ethan had gone after Mason. She whispered a prayer for his safety. How had she not seen it? Mason hadn't even been a blip on her suspect list.

What a blind, trusting fool she'd been.

Lost in the swirl of thought, she didn't register the dull clunk until a heavy weight fell across her.

Her eyes flew open.

Dustin lay sprawled over her, limp and unmoving. Above them stood the big guy, a pistol raised.

Had he shot Dustin?

No, she hadn't heard a gunshot. And there was no blood. He must've used the gun to knock Dustin out.

Sienna tried to shove him off, but he was too heavy, and she was still too weak. Another try. He didn't budge.

Then suddenly, Dustin was wrenched aside like a rag doll, and the big guy was reaching for her.

In one motion, he yanked her upright by the arm, stooped and slung her over his shoulder like she weighed nothing. His shoulder dug hard into her stomach. She doubted complaining would get her relocated.

She'd come too close to dying these past two weeks. More times than she wanted to count.

She'd almost died in the fire tonight. Each time, God had sent Ethan to rescue her. But he wasn't here now. Ethan was chasing Mason——the man behind it all. The man responsible for every sad, broken moment of the last six years. The man who had sent this behemoth to silence her.

Sienna blinked back tears. Forced herself to stay calm.

Testing a breath, she was grateful when it slid smoothly into her lungs. In the distance, sirens wailed.

Would they be too late?

The big guy didn't seem to care that law enforcement was on the way. He just kept walking, wordless, carrying her like a sack of grain. But he hadn't noticed when he'd hauled her off the ground that she'd grabbed the small oxygen tank.

Please, Father. Help me.

She'd never deliberately hurt anyone. But this was survival.

Holding her breath, she tightened her grip and brought the tank down hard on his skull.

The force of the blow dropped him instantly, all six-plus feet of him hitting the dirt in a graceless heap.

They crashed down together. Pain splintered through her as the ground slammed into her. She realized something too late: she hadn't thought through her moment of bravery.

The beat of the gelding's hooves thundered beneath Ethan as he leaned low in the saddle, eyes locked on the dark silhouette ahead. Mason was riding full tilt toward the helipad. If he reached it, he'd vanish into the night.

The moon cast silver streaks across the open field, and up ahead, Mason's horse stumbled on uneven ground.

Only yards away, a sleek black helicopter sat waiting, rotors beginning to spin. The low *whump-whump-whump* pulsed through the ground.

Mason glanced back, saw Ethan closing in and kicked his horse harder.

Ethan pushed the gelding, closing the gap.

"Don't do it, Mason!" he shouted over the rush of wind and the rising grumble of blades. "You're not getting away!"

Mason slowed, preparing to dismount and run for the chopper.

Ethan wasn't going to give him the chance.

He stood in the stirrups, heart pounding, and launched from

the saddle—his shoulder slamming into Mason's ribs and driving them both to the ground.

They hit hard, tumbling in the grass. Mason twisted, trying to fight him off, but Ethan had years of training—and six years' worth of reasons to end this.

He wrestled one of Mason's arms behind his back and planted a knee between his shoulder blades, pinning him.

"Stay down." He tightened his grip, every muscle locked. "It's over."

Finally, he was arresting the man who'd tried to have him killed. The one who'd forced Sienna to leave him. Who'd sent people to silence her. Who nearly destroyed everything Ethan loved and cherished.

And it felt good.

"Mason Blake." He pulled his cuffs from his belt. "You're under arrest for conspiracy to commit murder, arson, attempted homicide and fraud. You have the right to remain silent."

Mason bucked against him, breath heaving. "You have no idea who you're dealing with."

Ethan snapped the cuffs around both wrists, the metal locking into place with finality. "I know *exactly* who I'm dealing with."

Mason twisted his head, eyes gleaming with contempt. "You think this ends here? I'll make you regret this. You'll lose everything you care about."

Ethan stood, dragging Mason up with him.

"I already did." He propelled Mason forward, walking him to the horse. "Six years ago. Because of you."

In the distance, flashing lights drew closer as sirens echoed through the hills. Mason spat threats under his breath, but Ethan didn't respond.

He'd already won the only battle that mattered.

Sienna was back. He loved her, and he trusted her to love him back. It was time to let go of the past completely.

God had given him a second chance with Sienna. And he had a son he was going to help raise.

Thank You, Lord. Thank You.

The flashing lights bathed the ranch yard in pulses of red and blue, and the air was rich with the acrid scent of smoke. Deputies were loading the big guy into the back of a cruiser, while the fire crews doused the stable block, containing the fire.

Dustin sat on the open tailgate of the ambulance, an EMT shining a penlight into his eyes. He gave Sienna a thumbs-up when he caught her watching, his sheepish grin taking the edge off the bruise forming on his forehead.

Sienna sat inside the ambulance, a blanket around her shoulders, the oxygen mask now resting in her lap. She didn't need it anymore, she could breathe. It had been a mistake to underestimate how high off the ground she'd been when she swung the oxygen tank and knocked the big guy out. He'd crashed down, taking her with him.

Whether it was the smoke inhalation or the fall that made her black out, she didn't know. But she came to with an oxygen mask on her face, EMTs around her and a deputy snapping cuffs on the big guy as he started to stir.

Rescue crews had arrived within minutes of her knocking herself out. Dustin had already come around, sporting a lump on the back of his head from the butt of the big guy's gun and a bruise on his forehead from hitting the ground, but he'd been clearheaded enough to inform the medics and law enforcement about what had happened.

Ethan had been gone a while, and she anxiously watched for him to return.

And then she saw him.

He rode into the yard like a hero in a scene torn from the pages of a Western romance—dusty, smoke-streaked, jaw set and commanding as ever. Mason's body was slumped across the saddle in front of him, hands cuffed behind his back.

Ethan swung down, handed Mason off to a waiting deputy, turned and locked his eyes onto hers like she was the only person in the world. She threw off the blanket and jumped down from the ambulance. Before she could take a step, he was there, his arms wrapping around her. She sank into him, her hands fisting in the fabric of his shirt.

"You're safe now," he whispered against her hair. "It's over."

There was so much she wanted to say, but her throat closed around the emotion swelling inside her. So she simply clung to him. They stood like that, holding each other for a long time. Then, finally, she raised her head, met Ethan's eyes.

"I never wanted to leave you. I'm sorry for all the hurt I caused. I love you, Ethan, and I'll never leave you again."

He drew back slightly and brushed her hair from her face. "I know you'll never willingly leave me. But if you do, I'll come after you. Because I'm so deeply in love with you, Si, I'll never let you go again without a fight."

"Will you ever be able to forgive me?"

"I already have." He brushed his thumb over her cheek. "Marry me, Sienna. Let's be a family."

Overwhelming joy bloomed in her chest. Tears welled, spilled silently down her cheeks, yet she couldn't stop smiling. "We *are* a family." He'd always been her family.

"Then let's make it official." He reached for the clasp at the back of her neck, gently unfastening the chain. The engagement ring slid free into his palm. "You do realize…" he gave her his most devastatingly gorgeous smile "…we never actually broke off our engagement."

He took her left hand and slipped the princess-cut sapphire onto her finger, where it belonged. "I love you, Si. I've never stopped. It's always ever been only you. Wear my ring again.

Marry me as soon as we can make it happen. I never want to be without you by my side."

Sienna stared up at him, tears misting her vision. "I love you, Ethan. In my heart, I've always been married to you." She rose onto her toes, meeting him halfway. "I can't wait to be your wife."

Ethan's mouth found hers in a kiss that stole what little breath she had left. It was deep and sure and reverent, like he was memorizing her, pouring six years of love into a single moment. He held her face in his hands, thumbs brushing tears from her cheeks as his lips moved over hers with aching tenderness. The warmth of him, the strength, the quiet intensity—everything about this kiss felt like coming home.

She melted into him, her fingers sliding into his hair, holding on like he was the only thing tethering her to solid ground.

And maybe he was.

Six years of pain, of longing, of love bottled up and buried, broke free in that kiss. He kissed her like he'd waited forever, and she kissed him like she was reclaiming the years they'd lost. The world around them faded. The chaos, the lights, the noise— it all blurred and fell away. There was only this. Only them.

When he finally drew back, his breath was uneven and so was hers.

"I love you, Sienna." He rested his forehead against hers. "Always."

Fresh tears spilled over her lashes. God had been there all along, guiding her home...back to Ethan. They had a second chance at a future. She'd never let anything tear them apart again. "I love you, too, Ethan." She clung to him. "Always."

EPILOGUE

Two Years Later, Mother's Day

Sienna sat curled on the couch, her newborn daughter sleeping soundly against her chest. Ethan sat beside her, one arm around her shoulders, the other gently rubbing Amelia's tiny back. Not so long ago, Sienna hadn't known if Ethan could ever forgive her, if they could rebuild what they once had.

Now they were stronger than ever.

They'd married that first summer in a quiet ceremony on the ranch. James, Ethan's dad, had walked her down the aisle.

A lot had changed in two years.

Mason Blake, once the most powerful man in the state, was now serving a life sentence without parole. Jolene had cut a deal and testified against him in exchange for ten years in federal prison. Razor—the big guy—Mason's enforcer and the man who'd nearly taken Sienna's life, was now serving twenty years. Two more of Mason's hired men had been caught trying to flee the country and were sentenced shortly after.

During the investigation, authorities uncovered Jacob's original will buried in a locked safe, along with a file containing evidence of the bloodline fraud Mason had hidden. He'd forged Jacob's signature to create a false version, seizing control of the ranch for himself. Worse, he'd used Jacob's name to set up the shell account that paid for the semi that ran them off the road and framed a dead man to cover his tracks.

But the truth came out. The ranch had never belonged to Mason. Jacob had left it to Sienna's mom, Christine. Her mom had finally inherited what was rightfully hers and had moved back to Hope Haven to be near her grandchildren. She'd completed the equine rehab center, serving injured and neglected horses from across the region. Sienna was thrilled to be part of that.

With Christine, Grace and James nearby, there was never a shortage of eager babysitters. The grandparents doted on Nathan and Amelia so much, Sienna sometimes joked that if she wasn't careful, she might need to book an appointment just to hold her own children. This was the life she'd dreamed of for Nathan—being surrounded by abundant love from grandparents who treasured him and his sister.

Ethan looked down at her, love shining behind the quiet curve of his smile. "Happy Mother's Day, sweetheart."

She leaned into him, accepting his gentle kiss. "Thank you." She rested her head against his chest. "It really is."

Two years ago, she hadn't known if she and Ethan would ever find their way back to each other. Now, surrounded by the people she loved, she couldn't imagine being anywhere else. She had Ethan—her beloved husband. Her children. A family.

And, by the grace of God, she had peace.

This was what healing looked like.

This was home.

* * * * *

*Fall in love with stories where faith helps guide you
through life's challenges, and discover the promise
of a new beginning.*

*Look for six new releases every month, available wherever
Love Inspired Suspense books and ebooks are sold.*

Find more great reads at www.LoveInspired.com.

Dear Reader,

It began with a simple question: What if a woman sacrificed everything—including love—to protect the man she loved… and he never knew why she left? From that spark, Sienna and Ethan were born. Two people shaped by grief, faith and an enduring bond that neither time nor distance could erase.

Sienna's journey is one of courage—not just surviving danger but facing the past. Ethan, a man torn between betrayal and love, challenged me to explore what real forgiveness looks like. And Nathan, their son, became the heartbeat of the story.

Thank you for picking up this novel and stepping into Ethan and Sienna's world. I hope their story speaks to your heart as it did mine and reminds you of the power of second chances, the strength in surrender and the beauty of a God who never stops pursuing us.

Hugs,
Monique DeVere

Get up to 4 Free Books!

We'll send you 2 free books from each series you try
PLUS a free Mystery Gift.

Both the **Love Inspired**® and **Love Inspired**® **Suspense** series feature compelling novels filled with inspirational romance, faith, forgiveness and hope.

YES! Please send me 2 FREE novels from the Love Inspired or Love Inspired Suspense series and my FREE gift (gift is worth about $10 retail). I may cancel anytime by emailing ReaderServiceInfo@Harlequin.com or by calling 1-800-873-8635. If I don't cancel, I will receive 6 brand-new Love Inspired Larger-Print books or Love Inspired Suspense Larger-Print books every month and be billed just $7.19 each in the U.S. or $7.99 each in Canada. That is a savings of 20% off the cover price. It's quite a bargain! Shipping and handling is just 75¢ per book in the U.S. and $1.75 per book in Canada.* I understand that accepting the free books and gift places me under no obligation to buy anything—they are mine to keep for free no matter what I decide.

Choose one:
- ☐ **Love Inspired Larger-Print** (122/322 BPA G3CD)
- ☐ **Love Inspired Suspense Larger-Print** (107/307 BPA G3CD)
- ☐ **Or Try Both!** (122/322 & 107/307 BPA G3CE)

Name (please print)

Address ___ Apt. #

City ___ State/Province ___ Zip/Postal Code

Email: Please check this box ☐ if you would like to receive newsletters and promotional emails from Harlequin Enterprises ULC and its affiliates. You can unsubscribe anytime.

Mail to the **Harlequin Reader Service:**
IN U.S.A.: P.O. Box 1341, Buffalo, NY 14240-8531
IN CANADA: P.O. Box 603, Fort Erie, Ontario L2A 5X3

Want to explore our other series or interested in ebooks? Visit www.ReaderService.com or call 1-800-873-8635.

*Terms and prices subject to change without notice. Prices do not include sales taxes, which will be charged (if applicable) based on your state or country of residence. Canadian residents will be charged applicable taxes. Offer not valid in Quebec. This offer is limited to one order per household. Books received may not be as shown. Not valid for current subscribers to the Love Inspired or Love Inspired Suspense series. All orders subject to approval. Credit or debit balances in a customer's account(s) may be offset by any other outstanding balance owed by or to the customer. Please allow 4 to 6 weeks for delivery. Offer available while quantities last.

Your Privacy — Your information is being collected by Harlequin Enterprises ULC, operating as Harlequin Reader Service. For a complete summary of the information we collect, how we use this information and to whom it is disclosed, please visit our privacy notice located at https://corporate.harlequin.com/privacy-notice. Notice to California Residents—Under California law, you have specific rights to control and access your data. For more information on these rights and how to exercise them, visit https://corporate.harlequin.com/california-privacy. For additional information for residents of other U.S. states that provide their residents with certain rights with respect to personal data, visit https://corporate.harlequin.com/other-state-residents-privacy-rights.

LIRLIS2603